Detective Snyder strode into the shop...

His broad shoulders anchored a fit man with dark hair and dark eyes. Looking to be just over six feet tall, the detective filled the doorway. His sunglasses hid whatever he was thinking, which Kate was pretty sure began and ended with the words *annoying woman*.

He slid onto one of the bar stools and set a folder beside him. He had a nice profile, she realized, with sharp features dominated by his chocolate-brown eyes. In another life, he might be the kind of guy she'd date, but in this life, she was too consumed with righting the wrongs of her small town to even consider dating someone else.

"Is that my folder?" she asked.

"You get right down to business, I see." A smile flickered on his face. "That's one thing we have in common."

"When a missing girl needs to be found, whether someone took her or...worse, I don't want to waste a second."

Shirley Jump is an award-winning, *New York Times*, *Wall Street Journal*, Amazon and *USA TODAY* bestselling author who has published more than eighty books in twenty-four countries. Her books have received multiple awards and kudos from authors such as Jayne Ann Krentz, who called her books "real romance," and Jill Shalvis, who called her book "a fun, heartwarming small-town romance that you'll fall in love with." Visit her website at shirleyjump.com for author news and a booklist, and follow her on Facebook at Facebook.com/shirleyjump.author for giveaways and deep discussions about important things like chocolate and shoes.

Books by Shirley Jump

Harlequin Special Edition

The Stone Gap Inn

The Marriage Rescue
Their Unexpected Christmas Wish
Their Last Second Chance
The Family He Didn't Expect

Visit the Author Profile page
at Harlequin.com for more titles.

AFTER SHE VANISHED

SHIRLEY JUMP

LOVE INSPIRED
INSPIRATIONAL ROMANCE

LOVE INSPIRED®
INSPIRATIONAL ROMANCE

Recycling programs
for this product may
not exist in your area.

ISBN-13: 978-1-335-42610-9

After She Vanished

For questions and comments about the quality of this book, please contact us at CustomerService@Harlequin.com.

Love Inspired
22 Adelaide St. West, 41st Floor
Toronto, Ontario M5H 4E3, Canada
www.LoveInspired.com

Printed in U.S.A.

Beloved, let us love one another:
for love is of God; and every one that
loveth is born of God, and knoweth God.
—*1 John* 4:7

To my daughter,
the smartest, most amazing woman I've ever met.
I loved you before I even met you.

Chapter One

The small chrome desk lamp provided the only light in the cramped eight-by-ten room, a dimness Kate had long ago become accustomed to, almost comforted by. The lamp cast a pale puddle on the scratched desk and a dark spear of shadow that stretched to the corner of the wooden surface. A now-cold cup of orange blossom tea sat on a scuffed coaster, forgotten while she hurried to get the words out, to tell the story before anyone stopped listening.

This was Kate McAllister's favorite place, tucked in her home office with a microphone and her notes. It was just her and the facts, and an invisible audience listening in their cars, out on their runs or while they did dishes. For three years, she'd poured almost everything she had into the *Forgotten Victims* podcast she'd created. At first, as a way to keep Luke's case in the news, then as a way to keep his memory alive, and now, she supposed she did it because it helped her remember she wasn't alone.

Even after the man who had murdered her fiancé had been caught and put in prison, Kate kept telling the stories of the dead and forgotten. She'd been deluged with emails and messages begging her to take on cases that had been stored on shelves in the basements of police departments. And so she'd made it her mission to be their voice, one case at a time, one victim at a time.

Sleep had become a memory, given how many hours Kate spent awake. A predawn alarm to get her to the coffee shop she owned for an eight-, sometimes ten-hour shift there, then home for research and recording. She couldn't count the number of times she'd fallen asleep at her desk or downed a full pot of coffee just to make it through the morning. But every sleepless night and exhausting day was all worth it—every last waking minute—if it meant closure for the people who were hurting.

"We're starting a new season at *Forgotten Victims*," she said into the dynamic microphone she'd bought last year. That small piece of technology had been an investment, but it produced a richer sound than she could ever create on the cheap headset she'd started out recording with, back when she didn't know anything about podcasting. Her own words were a muffled redundancy coming from the soft ear coverings. "This time, we're journeying into the woods of Maggie Valley, where a teenage girl disappeared without a trace just before the Blue Ridge Music Festival. There's a family who is hurting out there, listeners, a family who desperately needs answers. I hope you can help."

She paused, took in a breath then picked up the pad of paper containing the notes she'd pulled together so far. What she hadn't received from Grace Ridge, Lily's mother, she'd gleaned from newspaper accounts and internet searches, doing her own legwork because she was still waiting on her Freedom of Information Act request. The administration of the Fordham, North Carolina police department had ignored her repeated inquiries, as if digging out a dusty box was too much work. She'd had an acrimonious relationship with the PD ever since Luke's body had been found. Well, there'd also been the incident last summer, which hadn't really been her fault.

The detectives didn't like someone—especially someone they deemed a wannabe crime investigator— asking questions and demanding answers, and she'd been there, nearly every day, hounding the cops. The FOIA guaranteed Kate, as a citizen, not to mention a journalist with a degree from University of North Carolina–Chapel Hill to boot, access to at least some of the files—but the police department could take their sweet time in delivering the information to her.

The small Fordham police department didn't seem all that motivated to help her. After all, the Ridge case had been cold for a long time, chalked up to yet another troubled teen, and except for the parents of Lily Ridge, Kate was pretty sure she was the only person looking into what had happened to the sixteen-year-old. At some point, she'd been labeled a runaway and the file on Lily had been, for all intents and purposes, closed.

"Lily was about to start her junior year in high school when she disappeared," Kate said. "She was full of hope and promise, and a dream to be a veterinarian someday. Her mother's Taurus and her purple backpack were found along the road in Soco Gap…" Kate paused, took a breath. Even now, three years later, the mention of that road caused a hitch in Kate's chest. If she closed her eyes, she could still see Luke's body, crumpled beside his car, the crimson pool of blood beneath his head.

There were days when the pain of that loss was a sharp knife in her side, when her heart broke for all Luke had missed, all he would never do. Days when she was angry with God for taking away the man she loved, the future they never had and the son his parents now mourned. It had taken a long time for her to let go of that grief, to stop being mad at God and start seeing His grace, and to move on, but she had never forgotten. So she kept on telling herself that the best thing—and only thing—she could do was keep talking so that no more families went through what she had.

"There was no other trace of Lily along that road, except for a set of footprints in the mud beside her car. It's been almost three years since Lily disappeared, and while I know this will be a challenging case, I can't help but try to bring some justice and answers to Lily's family."

She went on to talk about the page on her website that would be dedicated to Lily's case, something she had started when she began investigating Luke's disappearance. At first, the online vault of memories and details had been a way for her to keep all of her data together. Then, as interest in the podcast picked up, the audience began doing their own investigations, peppering her with tips and information. A crowdsourced murder investigation of sorts. That had led her to Luke's missing car, sitting in John David Wheatly's backyard, about a quarter mile off the road that wound through Soco Gap.

By all rights, she should have called the police department before acting. But there'd been months of frustration in dealing with Detective James Snyder, who seemed to find a million other things to do besides investigate a murder in his own town. He'd brushed her theories off a dozen times and probably would again.

She'd sat at the end of Wheatly's driveway having this internal debate for a long time before she called Snyder. She'd been so blinded by her grief that she didn't even think about how stupid it was to be less than a hundred feet from the house where a murderer sat on his couch, with two guns by his side. Wheatly could have killed her, could have taken her hostage, but he didn't. He said later that he'd sat and watched her watch him, because he knew there was no point in fighting the inevitable.

The risk had been worth it because now, Wheatly was in prison and maybe Luke could rest in peace.

Kate had no doubt God had led her to the answers and to that driveway, pointing her in the direction of justice, and because of that, her faith was stronger than it had ever been. Even as he had been hauled off to jail, Wheatly claimed he'd been framed and that he'd had no idea where the car came from or how it ended up parked outside his house, just one among dozens of junkers that Wheatly had collected or others dumped there, thinking Wheatly's run-down property was abandoned. Wheatly continued to protest his innocence and file appeals from jail. It didn't matter. Kate had some answers, and some would have to be enough. Wheatly could just rot where he was for the rest of his life.

"If you followed season one of *Forgotten Victims*, you'll know that my fiancé Luke Winslow was murdered around the same time and in an area very close to where Lily disappeared. Maybe that's why this case means so much to me and why I feel so compelled to help Lily's family. I know that season two didn't end as we all had thought, but our efforts did get the Fordham Police Department to do a better investigation into the death of Elaine Reynolds." Kate paused. The Reynolds case had nearly made her quit the podcast, quit everything. She'd been so convinced that Elaine had been murdered and had talked about the mystery of where Elaine's body might be for weeks. Fans from all over the area had driven to Fordham that summer, poking around the town, asking questions. Twice, the captain of the police department called Kate in and asked her to stop broadcasting. She'd refused.

She'd just been *so sure*. And wrong, it turned out, when Elaine was found a few days later, a victim of a suicide who had ended her life in the woods high above Soco Gap. The blood, the disarray in the house, the lack of any trace of Elaine…it had all seemed so clear that it was murder, until Detective Snyder found her journals and said what she'd written pointed to a suicide. Elaine had been depressed for months after the end of a relationship and had made two attempts at ending her life in the months prior to her death, all signs that came to the same conclusion. Either way, the podcast had brought resolution to Elaine's family, who'd been frantic about her disappearance.

This case, though, was different. Kate knew in her gut that Lily wasn't a runaway. Except…a part of her doubted even that gut feeling. What if she was wrong? It wouldn't be the first time.

Kate shook her head. *Focus on the facts. That's the path to answers.* "I hope, dear listeners, that we can find the truth once again. Tune in next week, when we'll start digging into the details of the case."

She clicked Stop on the recorder, turned off her mic and set the heavy headphones on the desk. Kate's back ached from being on her feet on a concrete floor all day, then sitting in the rickety desk chair for the last half of her day. She rose, stretching as she did, and realized the sun had gone down sometime while she was recording. It wasn't the first time she'd missed the end of a day, and it likely wouldn't be the last. Running her late mother's coffee shop in downtown Fordham and recording the podcast when she got home meant Kate had very few free daylight hours. She didn't go out with her friends that often, didn't date. Some would say she was using all of this as an excuse to avoid getting involved, and maybe those people were right.

Once upon a time, she'd spent those hours hiking the trails of Maggie Valley with Luke and his mixed mutt of a dog, Harley. They'd gone on picnics and camping trips and impromptu explorations in a kayak. There were days when those moments seemed so far in the past, it was as if the days had been lived by someone else. In Kate's head and heart, there was a clear divide between before Luke died and after Luke died. And an eon of heartache in the wake of that death.

Jenn, Kate's roommate, looked up as Kate emerged from her makeshift office. "One of these days, I'm going to find you living inside that closet you call a studio. All you need is a hot plate and an air mattress."

"I could get more work done if I did that." Kate grinned. Harley scrambled to his feet and pressed his body against Kate's leg. She gave Harley a good ear rub, and the mutt thumped his tail in gratitude. The Lab-shepherd-something mix had been glued to her side ever since Luke died. For a long time, Harley had been the steady furry friend who caught her tears. Now he'd become her best friend and her shadow. "Thanks for the idea."

Jenn unfolded her long legs and got to her feet. Taller than Kate by a couple inches, Jenn was the kind of woman that Kate's grandmother would have called willowy. She had waist-length black hair and big green eyes, and if she was anyone other than Jenn, Kate would probably envy all that gorgeousness in one package.

The true measure of Jenn's beauty came in the form of compassion and kindness. She worked as a vet tech in town and adopted pretty much anything that was orphaned, from the scraggly plants drying in the sun at the hardware store to an injured butterfly on the windowsill. And most of all, a wounded, heartbroken best friend who could barely crawl out of bed after her fiancé's murder. There were many days when Kate was sure God had dropped Jenn and Harley into her life simply to save her from her grief. Kate had lived in town before moving to this apartment, one she had thought she would share with her husband. Jenn had become Kate's roommate a little over a year ago, when Jenn's lease was up, the two of them needing not just a place they could afford, but a place that wasn't so…empty.

"I worry about you," Jenn said. "Besides, somebody's got to play fetch with Harley so I can get caught up on *The Bachelor*."

At the sound of the word *fetch*, the dog bounded off to retrieve one of the dozens of stuffed toys that littered the carpet. Kate laughed. "I'm glad I have a purpose in life." She tossed the stuffed rabbit across the living room. It skittered under the breakfast table and Harley scrambled after it, nearly upsetting the chairs.

Jenn's features sobered. "You know you have more than that, Kate, right? What you're doing on that show…it's pretty incredible. Just don't lose yourself like you did before. Okay?"

During the months she'd worked on the first season, Kate had been pulled into the darkness many times as she recounted what had happened to Luke, week after week. She'd thought of pulling the plug on the podcast a thousand times, but in the end, her quest to bring closure to Luke's mother, and to Kate's own heart, kept her returning to the mic. And when the Elaine Reynolds disappearance went sideways, Kate had questioned her entire purpose in life. It had thrown her into a deep depression, compounded by all the grief she'd been avoiding by working so many hours.

"I won't. Not this time. I promise." Kate said the words, but already she could feel her heart breaking for Lily's family, because she knew their pain, knew that justice would only heal the wound so much. Answers would help, and so would the knowledge that hundreds of other people cared, but that could only happen if the podcast got some traction. Kate needed to get that police report and start making some progress on the case. Maybe then her mind would stop spinning.

Jenn's phone dinged. She stretched across the couch and unplugged it from the charger, then made a face. "It's the animal shelter. They need someone to cover Marcie's shift tonight. I know we were planning on a girls' night but—"

"It's fine. It's fine." Kate waved off Jenn's apology. Truth be told, Kate would rather be here, digging through her files and burrowing into the secrets the internet held on Lily's case. "I'll order in and do my nails and binge-watch too much TV."

"Sure you will." Jenn gave her a hug, then drew back and met Kate's gaze. "Promise me you will take at least an hour of time for yourself tonight."

"Pinky swear."

Jenn gave her friend a look of misgiving. She opened her mouth as if she was going to say more, but instead she just shook her head and headed out of the living room.

As soon as Jenn was out of sight, Kate booted up her laptop, feeling a twinge of guilt that she'd promised something that likely wouldn't happen. The chances of her taking even five minutes of me-time were miniscule. There was simply too much at stake. And so Kate dug in for another long night in front of the screen.

Without much to go on, googling for clues meant spending hours chasing down whispers on social media. Many of Lily's friends still posted about her, especially as the anniversary of her disappearance neared. By digging deeper into her timeline and friends list, and then the feeds of the people they were friends with, Kate was starting to build a social circle for Lily—which could include the person who was responsible for her disappearance. Or it could be a colossal waste of time. Either way, Kate couldn't leave any stone unturned.

Kate sent another message to Lily's best friend, Ashley. Many of Lily's friends returned Kate's requests for information, but none of them had been as close to Lily as Ashley had been. So far, Ashley had ignored Kate's requests to talk about the day her friend disappeared. Maybe she was afraid, or maybe she truly didn't have anything to share.

When Jenn came back into the room, out of her yoga pants and changed into jeans and a T-shirt centered by the shelter's logo, she glanced at Kate, buried in notebooks and research, and shook her head. "One hour, okay?"

"Uh-huh." But Kate was immersed in her work and barely heard Jenn's words or the closing of the apartment door.

Three hours later, Kate slathered some peanut butter and jelly on two pieces of bread, called it dinner then carried her pile of research into her bedroom. While the TV played something she didn't watch, Kate read and made notes until her eyes grew too heavy to stay open, and then she fell asleep among the stack of papers.

That was far easier than facing the fact that her life had narrowed into a world where all she did was work and worry.

Mack Snyder strode into the Fordham Police station a little after seven in the morning. Most days, he was the first one to arrive and the last one to leave, a work ethic he'd picked up from his father, and his grandfather before him, both driven men who didn't believe in the word *quit*. Even though Mack had made detective two years ago, he still felt this overpowering need to prove himself as a worthy representative of the Snyder legacy to the other more seasoned men in the department.

And especially to his family.

Some psychiatrist would undoubtedly say it was because of his father, who had retired last year, and who still remained the gold standard for everyone at the police department. When people talked about Captain James Snyder, it was in the hushed tones of respect and awe. Mack loved his dad, but sometimes it was tough to live in the shadow of someone who towered so high over ordinary people. Especially when that someone judged his own son more harshly than any criminal he had put behind bars.

Mack's father was the first person he told about the promotion. James Snyder had scoffed and said simply, *We'll see what kind of job you do.* That offhand criticism had eaten at every doubt and fear that Mack had rumbling around in his brain and made him a hundred times more determined to prove his father wrong.

Mack crossed to his desk and started flipping through the reports that had piled up over the weekend. He'd gone to Charleston for a couple days to visit his mother, a long-overdue visit that had also put him far behind at work. She was a nervous, busy woman, who had issues with everything from the supermarket forgetting to pack eggs in her order, to her car needing oil. But she loved him fiercely and had been the one person who supported his decision to go into police work. She'd encouraged him to get his criminal justice degree and to take extra classes in forensic science.

She'd divorced his father when Mack was seventeen and moved away from Fordham. He had to admit that she seemed happier, more centered and calmer without the harsh, critical James Snyder in her life.

Mack had expected the investigative work to be challenging, exciting. But honestly, nothing really bad ever happened in Fordham. Yes, there'd been the murder of Luke Winslow, but that had been solved within a matter of weeks, and one disappearance last year that had turned out to be a fiasco for the force, but a single death hardly made for a crime spree. Nevertheless, there were often more cases than manpower, mostly burglaries and vandalism. Only three people comprised the Fordham investigative unit, which meant Mack and the other two detectives were especially busy during the spring and summer months when the beautiful valley was overrun with tourists.

An hour later, Chief Richmond came into the office, juggling a Venti black coffee in one hand and a pile of paperwork in the other. Tall, broad-shouldered and with a tight buzz cut that never seemed to grow any longer, the chief had been a cop for as long as

Mack had known him. He didn't bend rules or cross lines or try to micromanage the men under his command. To Mack, the chief was sometimes a little too hands-off, especially when the department needed direction and a nudge. But he was a good man, and Mack figured whatever his management style, Richmond clearly valued the town and the department above everything else.

"Snyder." The Chief gave Mack a small nod. "You're in early. Again."

"Gotta get up earlier than the criminals, Chief," Mack said. He and the chief exchanged the same conversation they always did, and just as he did the day before and all the days before that, Mack skipped the small talk and got right to work. "I've been going over the hardware store burglary report. Something is bugging me about that eyewitness account. I think I'll head out and interview him again today."

"Okay. But only after you deal with that woman at reception." Richmond thumbed toward the glass area just beyond the cubicles.

"She's back again?" Mack ran a hand through his hair and let out a sigh. At least once a week, Kate McAllister came into the station to ask about her FOIA request. Mack was in no hurry to give an amateur sleuth information. All she was going to do was put him even further behind. That mess with the Elaine Reynolds investigation last year had the police spending too much time chasing down that podcaster's "helpers". And now she was claiming she was the one who solved the murder of Luke Winslow, because she'd been an idiot and confronted the killer herself. It was a lot of good police work that put the pieces together with John David Wheatly, not a Good Samaritan thinking she was a detective.

Kate's new case, the disappearance of Lily Ridge, was an open-and-shut case. Mack had read the file the day the FOIA request crossed his desk. Mack's father had conducted the investigation just before he retired, and everything in the notes pointed to a runaway. There was even an eyewitness who had spotted the girl in Florida. Mack knew his father and knew he wasn't the kind of man to take his job lightly or make mistakes.

Kate McAllister apparently didn't agree. She ran a coffee shop downtown, a place he used to frequent because the strawberry scones were better than his grandma's, until he turned on the radio one day and heard her supposed true-crime podcast. The last season of her show had brought tourists from neighboring states, all thinking they could solve a murder while they were on spring break. Those meddling people had almost killed a man with their traipsing through the town, desperate to find that one witness who would unearth the truth behind a murder that had never happened. The whole town had been on edge that chaotic, tense summer, and the department had looked like bumbling fools unable to contain a woman with a microphone and a bunch of looky-loo tourists.

The last thing Mack wanted was a repeat of that fiasco because it had made the force look bad, and made him look like an idiot who didn't deserve the badge in his wallet. Ever since, he'd been trying to prove himself as a worthy addition to the team, and engaging with this podcaster was not the way to do it.

Mack started to protest, but the chief put up a hand. "Listen, Snyder, it's in our best interests to cooperate with the media. Tourist season is starting up and we don't need people thinking we're running around here like the Keystone Cops. Last year, the *Tribune* hopped on that comment of McAllister's saying we had flubbed the investigation. I got calls for a month about that one, even though it turned out that podcaster was completely off base. Don't even get me started on the bad press after she did that story on the Winslow autopsy."

Luke Winslow's autopsy had been done too quickly by a sloppy coroner who'd wanted to close the file instead of being late for dinner reservations. Once upon a time, Doc Josephs had been great at his job, but as the years piled on, that commitment to covering all the details began to slip. One mistake became two, which became a botched autopsy three years ago. Mack's dad had known Josephs most of his life and was the only reason Josephs kept his job after the Winslow case.

Three years later, Fordham had had enough issues with Doc Josephs, which had resulted in him being fired last week. Mack had never particularly liked the man. Something about Josephs just rubbed Mack the wrong way. He was too hurried, too nervous, too…messy. Every time Mack went in his office, Josephs's desk was covered with papers, and it took him ten minutes just to find a pen. Maybe it was early dementia or work exhaustion, but the once meticulous Josephs had become less and less so with each case he worked on, and eventually it had gotten to the point where there were no words James Snyder could use to defend his old football teammate.

"The new coroner won't make those mistakes," Mack said. "But you're right. We should do a little image building."

"What was it your dad always said? Never hurts to make sure your uniform is shiny. You never know when you'll be under the spotlight." Chief Richmond gave him a nod. "I trust you to handle it well, and keep it quiet that we are giving the last few autopsies Josephs did a second look."

The vote of confidence warmed Mack. He ducked out of his cubicle and headed down the hall to the reception area. Even before he entered the room, he could see Larry, the front desk sergeant, arguing with the coffee shop owner.

"Ma'am, I'm doing all I can. You're just going to have to be patient. I'm sure the detective—" Larry turned, saw Mack, and his entire body sagged with relief. "Detective Snyder will help you out."

Kate McAllister pivoted toward Mack. Lines of frustration marred her pretty face, and a slight flush filled her cheeks. She had her blond hair in a messy ponytail, with several strands escaping and curling along her neck. Bright green eyes met his, sharp and annoyed. "Detective Snyder. I'm so glad to finally speak to you. I've left several messages for you over the last two months."

"Seventeen to be exact." He cleared his throat, remembered his promise to the lieutenant. "Ms. McAllister, I'm afraid my answer is the same. I don't have the time to—"

"Do I need to get Judge Harris involved?" She propped a fist on her hip. "By law, you have to comply with my FOIA request, something I'm sure you know. I've been more than patient, Detective. I have a right to this information and so does the public."

"The same public that ran through town like a herd of elephants in a china shop and nearly got someone killed?" Mack drew in a deep breath and forced himself to settle. Why did this woman rattle him so easily? "Now, if you'll excuse me, I'm late for—"

"Very late handing over those files. This is not an optional request, Detective. The law states—"

"I know the law, Ms. McAllister." He shook his head. *I trust you to handle it well.* The lieutenant had made it clear Mack was supposed to cooperate with Kate. This was the opposite of being cooperative. "Ma'am, I have actual police work to do this morning." He held up a hand, cutting off her protest. "But if you can wait until eleven or so, I can bring the file to you."

Her eyes widened in surprise, and in an instant, the antagonism vanished from her features. When she wasn't yelling at him, Kate McAllister was actually quite pretty. "Thank you, Detective Snyder. I'll be at work at the coffee shop."

"I know. I've been there many times."

"Oh yes. Of course. I've seen you in there before."

"It's the scones, really. I…" He cleared his throat before he engaged in the very kind of small talk he despised. "I'll see you at eleven, ma'am."

"See you then." She started to walk away, then turned back. "And, Detective, if you promise never to call me ma'am again, the next scone is on me." Then she flashed him a smile, a fleeting but dazzling gesture that lit up her whole face. A moment later, she was gone, and it took Mack a solid twenty seconds to remember where exactly he'd been in such a hurry to go.

Chapter Two

The rich, dark scent of coffee filled the air of The Corner Cup, like a welcoming neighbor throwing open her door on a bright spring morning. Kate poured a steaming cup of Colombian roast, added a little creamer and a sprinkle of sugar then took a seat on the bar stool behind the counter. She had approximately forty-five seconds to enjoy her coffee before the regulars started trickling through the door.

The shop was small, maybe fifteen by sixty feet, with a counter, a few tables and a couple of battered love seats arranged in front of coffee tables stacked high with board games and jigsaw puzzles. The gray shiplap walls gave the shop an air of cabin in the woods, a nice match to the forest green chairs and ebony wood tables. When Kate's mother opened the shop thirty years ago, she'd intended it to be a part-time venture, a way to make a little extra money in the mornings before work and on the weekends. But within two years, the shop's clientele had grown so large, Kate's mother quit her job and expanded the hours from early morning to late afternoon. Kate had spent more than one afternoon doing homework at this very counter.

Then her mother died eight years ago, and Kate had come home, skipping her college graduation ceremony and an internship at the *Charlotte Observer*, to keep the business afloat. Her father had made one thing clear at the funeral—that he had no intention of running Mom's coffee shop, and if Kate wanted it, she had to take it over. Maybe it was some leftover childhood angst or a lesson in patience from God that kept her here, living in the same town as her father, a man who had never quite gotten far enough past his grief and bitterness to build a relationship with his only child.

Right on time, the bell over the door chimed and Ernie Lackner strode into the shop. Tall and lanky, Ernie had a penchant for baseball hats and an endless supply of striped mechanic shirts. He'd retired from the automotive repair shop he owned several years ago, passing the business on to a longtime employee, but he kept coming into the coffee shop every morning at the same time he always did.

"Morning, Kate." He tipped his hat and slid onto one of the stools at the counter.

"Morning, Ernie." She poured a cup of a dark, deep roast, then slid the ceramic cup over to him. "It's a beautiful day out there."

"Any day that I'm on this side of the lawn is a good day." He blew on the coffee, then took a sip and smiled. "Did you get the Ethiopian beans in again, those ones with the fancy name I can never remember?"

"Yirgacheffe, and of course I reordered them because I knew they were your favorite." She grinned as she grabbed the tongs and bent down to take a strawberry scone out of the case. She heated it for exactly ten seconds in the microwave, then gave it to Ernie.

He thanked her. "You remember my order every single time."

"That's because you order the same thing every single time." She laughed. "You're as predictable as a sunrise, Ernie."

"That's what my wife always says—'There are no surprises with you, husband. You're like an already opened Christmas gift.'"

"Well, I happen to think any Christmas gift is wonderful, so I'd take that as a compliment."

Ernie smiled. "That woman knows me well. She keeps me on my toes and makes every day a little sweeter. I miss her something fierce and I hope..." He clutched the mug in both hands.

Kate touched Ernie's sleeve. His wife had gone into the hospital three days ago after she fell and broke her hip. The surgery had gone well, but her recovery had been a bit rough. Mary Lackner was nearing eighty years old and was having trouble rebounding. "She's going to be just fine. We have her on the prayer list at church, and you know the power of prayer is amazing."

"I sure appreciate that." He gave her a watery smile, then covered for the emotion by taking another sip of coffee. "That church has been a godsend for us, sending me over so many meals, I think I could feed half the town for six months. My Mary couldn't drag me into that building with a team of oxen before all this happened, but I sure realized how much I need that support without her around to keep me in line." Ernie shrugged. "Some lessons you just learn too late, and then you do your best trying to make it right."

"Wise words." Kate turned away and busied herself with wiping countertops that were already clean. After Luke had died, the regrets that weighed on her shoulders had been part of the driving force to start the podcast. When they were dating, Luke had told her a hundred times that she needed to carve out a corner of the world that was hers alone, a spot that fulfilled the purpose God had created for her. But she'd always been too afraid to take those risks, to step outside the lines she'd kept around her life. *I hope you're proud of me, Luke.*

A few minutes later, Ernie said goodbye and headed to the hospital to see his wife. The coffee shop began to fill with the dozen or so customers that came in almost every morning. Men in suits on their way to work, harried moms returning from school drop-off, friendly neighbors who wanted to chat and a handful of elderly folks who liked to escape their empty homes and have some company. Kate greeted each one, filling the orders that were as familiar as her own name. The morning passed quickly, and as the clock ticked past ten, the shop began to empty out for the lull before the lunchtime rush.

She pulled yesterday's clean rack of mugs out of the dishwasher, then set today's dirty ones on another rack and pressed Start. As she wiped each one before tucking the sparkling mug away, Kate paused from time to time to scroll through her phone. The Facebook post she'd put on the podcast's page after she dropped the first episode was garnering some attention and comments. Most people expressed either sympathy for the family or outrage at the police department, but a few had intriguing comments that Kate wanted to investigate further.

Why did her parents let her be out there alone at such a young age?

What did she think was going to happen being out on that desolate road?

A girl like her deserved everything she got.

The last one had a chilling note to the words. Posted by someone named Wary Watcher, the words sent a shiver down Kate's spine. She clicked on the profile name, but it led her to a page of nothing. No cover photo, no posts and only a black circle for the profile photo. Whoever Wary Watcher was, it was going to take more than a few clicks to find the information. Either way, he was probably one of those living-in-his-mother's-basement internet trolls who just liked to stir up trouble.

The bell over the door dinged, and Detective Snyder strode into the shop, a man who had a presence everywhere he went. His broad shoulders anchored a fit man with dark hair and dark eyes. The detective's six feet or so of height filled the doorway. His sunglasses hid whatever he was thinking, which Kate was pretty sure began and ended with the words *annoying woman*.

"Ms. McAllister." He gave her a slight nod.

She grinned. "You didn't call me ma'am. We're already off to a good start."

He'd come into the shop all severe and buttoned up, but the joke made his features loosen. He slid onto one of the bar stools and set a folder beside him. "If that good start includes one of those strawberry scones, I'd have to agree."

"It's the least I can do." And it wouldn't hurt to keep the detective happy so he'd be more inclined to work with her. She selected the last strawberry scone, heated it for a few seconds then handed him the plate. "Do you want some coffee too?"

"Whatever you've got that's strong and plain, I'll take a cup of."

She filled a mug with Ernie's favorite Ethiopian roast and set that in front of the detective. He had a nice profile, she realized, with sharp features dominated by his chocolate-brown eyes. In another life, he might be the kind of guy she'd date, but in this life, she was too consumed with righting the wrongs of her small town to even consider dating someone else. And a part of her heart was still attached to Luke, in virtually everything she did. "Is that my folder?"

"You get right down to business, I see." A smile

flickered on his face. "That's one thing we have in common."

"When a missing girl needs to be found, whether someone took her or…worse, I don't want to waste a second of that talking about the weather."

His smile evaporated. Clearly, he didn't like her questioning the police department's conclusions about what happened to Lily Ridge. Maybe it was because his father had been the one to do the initial investigation and family loyalty trumped finding the truth

"I don't think you're going to find any bodies or any surprises in this file," he said. "It's very open-and-shut."

She took the folder from him and began flipping through the file. Several lines were blacked out, which meant the department had redacted some of the information. Frustration welled in her chest. How was she supposed to get to the truth without all the facts? "If Lily's case is so open-and-shut why isn't everything here?"

"Because we're protecting the privacy of citizens."

"Oh come on, Detective. Lily's family told you they were working with me to find answers that you couldn't, and they agree that there's more here than what the police are saying. You said yourself that the department deemed Lily a runaway. Why are you protecting anyone's identity if they would corroborate your version of the story?"

He bristled. "There are no versions, Ms. McAllister. There is only the truth, and the truth is that Lily Ridge left home on purpose."

"Even if that was so, why would her backpack be on the road?" A couple of customers glanced over at Kate, so she lowered her voice and leaned closer to the detective. "Why would her car be left behind?"

"Because she was leaving her old life behind. She was a troubled teenager, just getting over a breakup, fighting with her mom all the time. She probably didn't want one more battle with them. Her parents held the title on the car, so she couldn't resell it to fund her new life. The backpack was filled with schoolbooks and homework. If she's running away from home, she's not going to be showing up at Fordham High on Monday morning."

He made a valid point, but still, Kate couldn't believe that the girl had just run off without a word to her parents for three years, no matter how badly they fought. Everyone she'd talked to about Lily had said she wasn't the kind of girl to do that. "And her cell phone? She's never used it again after that day, and it's never been found."

"Because she didn't want to be found, Ms. McAllister. It happens. Teenagers fight with their parents, and they take off, and sometimes make foolish, stubborn decisions."

"She didn't just disappear. Someone took her, Detective."

"Look through that file and you'll see what I saw. Lily Ridge had a boyfriend who was more than a little sketchy. They broke up just a week or two before she disappeared. He took off around the same time as she did, and she probably hitched a ride with him. I'm sure they had a fight and he left her somewhere between here and Florida."

"Did you ask him if he did?" Lily's ex-boyfriend Alex Harmon was someone Kate hadn't been able to find yet. He didn't seem to have a social media presence, and she had no idea where he was living now.

"The case is three years old and has already been closed. There is no need to go chasing rabbits down trails that lead nowhere." He got to his feet. The subject was clearly closed. "Thank you for the coffee, ma'am."

The detective dropped a few dollars on the counter, then left the shop. Kate clutched the folder to her chest and vowed that Detective Snyder was not going to have the last word on Lily Ridge. The girl was out there somewhere, and it was up to Kate to bring her home. No matter how much effort that took or where the trail led her.

Mack smiled and nodded, then smiled and nodded some more. There were days when his job was filled with excitement and days when it was little more than paperwork and community relations. "Mrs. Piper, I'm not sure what you want me to do about this."

Antonia Piper's lips pinched and her gaze narrowed. She was an elderly woman who lived alone in a giant Georgian-style home on the edge of downtown. She was stubborn—which was why the road to the highway went around her house instead of through it—and she was a frequent caller on the department's emergency line. "Detective, you must be able to find it somehow. My rabbit statue is missing from my front yard, and I want it back."

"Ma'am, I'm afraid that isn't something that falls inside my purview. The value of the item, you said so yourself, is less than twenty dollars and—"

"It was *last season's* model. Do you know what that means, Detective? I can't get that same rabbit statue this season. I have to get the one with the green bow tie, not the yellow bow tie, and green does not match my garden decor."

As far as Mack could see, most of her garden was green, but he wasn't about to quibble with anyone about decorating, given that his apartment had been styled in Early Bachelor for most of his life. "Ma'am, I'm sure it was some kids messing around. I can't—"

"You need to police the teenagers in this town better, Detective Snyder. Why, I hear those hooligans at all hours of the night. They're laughing and talking and doing who knows what out on those sidewalks."

"We run extra patrols during tourist season, ma'am. I'll be sure to let the desk sergeant know we should send a car this way more often."

"And can you put out one of those A-P things on my statue? That little bunny is dear to my heart."

"Do you mean an APB? Ma'am, those are for missing persons, not statues." He could see Antonia readying another argument. He held up his notepad, filled with scribbles from the half-hour conversation he'd had about the cement rabbit. "But I have your information, and I'll ask the other officers to be on the lookout for..." He scanned the paper.

"Peter the Rabbit. Thank you, Detective. I appreciate you looking out for the citizens of Fordham."

"Just doing my job." He gave Antonia a wave, then headed back to his car. So far today, he'd accomplished pretty much nothing. The witness to the hardware store robbery had seen *a kinda blue car and a guy who might have been wearing a hat*, not exactly enough to do a lineup. There'd been Mrs. Piper and a couple other vandalism calls, but nothing major. Of course, he should be grateful that Fordham was so quiet as tourist season was beginning. He didn't want to wish trouble on this little town he'd been in all his life, but he also loved a challenge.

Kate McAllister was definitely a challenge, but Mack had no intentions of getting swept up into her theories. He could see their conversation today turning into a page-by-page debate of the Ridge file, and in the end, Mack was sure he would see the case just as his father had—a teenage runaway who had started a new life far from this town.

When he got back into his car, he saw a half-dozen messages filling the screen of his personal cell phone. Mack sighed and scrolled through the texts his mother had sent him just in the half hour he'd been talking about the missing Peter the Rabbit.

His mother was panicking about something again. There were days when she was perfectly fine, then others when it seemed like handling an ordinary day was too much. I need to talk to you. Call me when you can. Where are you? Why haven't you answered? I need to talk to you. It's important. Call me back. I tried calling you and went to voice mail. I need some help, and you're the only one I can ask.

Mack dialed his mother's number, one as familiar as his right hand, and braced himself. "What's wrong, Ma?"

"The furnace won't come on. I think I'm going to freeze to death tonight."

Mack checked the temperature reading on the dashboard. "Ma, it's seventy-two outside right now. You're not going to freeze to death."

"But it's cold in here. It's much colder in Charleston, you know. We're so much closer to the water."

He was about to argue that his mother lived more than a hundred miles from the Atlantic Ocean but already knew the argument would continue circling. "Put me on FaceTime and let me look at the thermostat."

"Okay, but you'll see that it's absolutely frigid in here. Where is that darn button? Oh, here it is." A close-up of his mother's chin came into view.

"Turn the camera around, Ma. Or press the flip button."

"You know I don't know how to use technology, Mack." The camera shook as she pressed the phone closer to the thermostat. The indoor temperature read seventy-four degrees, not even close to frigid.

"Okay, if you want to put the furnace on, you have to switch the thermostat to heat." His mother got overwhelmed by things she didn't understand, maybe because his father had handled everything to do with the house when they were married. "Slide the button to the left and under the word *Heat*." He waited while his mother muttered on the other end about the impossibility of the thermostat and how cold she was. Then he heard a soft click, as the thermostat in his mother's house came to life. "You got it now?"

"I do. But I'm not sure it'll work. It's been so long since I had the heat on and I'm worried the furnace is getting worn out."

"I'll check it the next time I come over."

"Do you promise?" The tremors in her voice echoed with doubt, anxiety. The fissure of guilt that ran through Mack's every vein opened a little wider. She was lonely and said often how much she missed having her kids underfoot because being a great mother had been her biggest purpose in life. He made a promise to himself to visit her again soon.

A tiny part of Mack, a part he refused to listen to, resented his father for leaving their fragile mother as easily as recycling a newspaper. He'd been cold and callous in the divorce, and his indifference had only made her anxiety worse. Maybe there were things beneath their marriage that Mack didn't know or understand, things that could explain why his father had acted that way. It wasn't a topic Mack ever brought up when he visited his father on Wednesday and Saturday nights, because the past was already gone, as Dad liked to say, and talking about it wouldn't change anything. Dad wasn't the type to get emotional or express anything as frivolous as regret, so Mack found himself doing twice as much as he probably should for his mother and sister, if only to make up for his father's coldness.

"Yes, I promise." He glanced at the pile of paperwork sitting on the seat of his car, waiting to be written, filed and dealt with. There was no way he could fit another trip to Charlotte into his schedule, not this week. "You could always ask Rachel to come out, Ma."

"Your sister is busy. She has work and that new husband."

He wanted to say he had work, too, but he knew that wouldn't make a difference. His mother played by old-school rules—men took care of the women in their families, especially their mothers. His sister worked part-time and had just celebrated her fifth anniversary with her "new" husband, and had the time to run between Charlotte and Fordham, but in his mother's eyes, all that responsibility rested on the shoulders of her son.

"I'll figure it out," Mack said. "I have to go, Ma."

She sighed. "You're always so busy. I never talk to you anymore. But fine. I'll let you go. Call me later?"

"Of course." After Mack hung up, he checked his work phone and saw ten more to-dos to add to tomorrow. Nothing major, but a lot of little investigations that often turned out to be ridiculously time-consuming. He put the car in gear, and instead of turning west to his apartment, he went east, winding through suburban neighborhoods that could have been copies of each other before finally arriving at a small yellow bungalow with a tidy yard and a white picket fence.

Rachel was kneeling on a plastic mat in front of the flower beds, nestling impatiens in the ground. She turned and gave her brother a wave as he got out of the car. At least once a week, Mack went to his sister's house for a home-cooked meal that didn't come out of a drive-through or a box. He liked her husband, who was a practicing attorney, well enough, and had always been close to his little sister. "Hey, Mack," she said. "You're a little early for Taco Tuesday."

"It's never too early for tacos." He dropped onto the top step of the front porch and watched his sister move on to the next fledgling plant. "Ma called me today."

"That's not exactly a news flash. She calls you every day. Sometimes several times in one day."

"This time, she's convinced her furnace is going to die any second now. She wants me to drive over there and take a look at it."

Rachel sat back on her knees and peered out at him from under the brim of her floppy hat. "You know the more you jump when she says how high, the worse it's going to get. Ma is really needy, and I hate to say it, but I think the thing she needs most is to learn how to be okay on her own."

"Rachel, she's set in her ways."

"And will continue to be unless you stop rescuing her over every little thing." Rachel tapped the plastic bottom of the next pot, releasing the pink flower.

She used the spade to clear a fresh hole before dropping the plant into the space. "I know you feel like it's your responsibility, but not everything has to sit on your shoulders just because Dad makes you feel guilty all the time. He didn't do his part when he was married to her, so he shouldn't criticize you at all."

"Yeah. I know." He drew in a breath of fresh spring air and let it settle in his chest for a moment. "Before we sit down to dinner, I wanted to talk to you about something."

Rachel stopped working and sat back. "Sure. What about?"

"You knew Kate McAllister in high school, right?"

"Yeah. Not super well but we had a few classes together and she was in my homeroom."

"Is she deluded or just ridiculously driven?" The blatant question was out before he could stop it.

Rachel laughed. "Definitely not crazy. Why?"

"She's been bugging me about the Lily Ridge case. She's convinced there was foul play, but Dad ruled it a runaway three years ago." Mack had worked parts of the case with his father but had mainly been kept in the station, checking bank statements and contacting other students in Lily's high school to see if they knew anything. All of the hands-on work had been handled by his father, keeping Mack from having much direct knowledge of the case.

Rachel didn't say anything for a minute. She shifted her gaze and moved on to the next impatiens in her basket. "Yeah, and Dad's always right." She muttered the words under her breath as she tapped soil around the plant.

"Dad was one of the best cops on the force, Rach. No one was as good at the job as he was."

Rachel sighed. "You have these rose-colored lenses when it comes to him. He isn't all sunshine and daisies, you know. And I doubt he was some kind of super cop at work, either. Everyone makes mistakes, including Dad."

"Maybe at home. But at work, he was a rock star." Maybe that was part of what had made Rachel's relationship with their father contentious. Mack and Dad had work to sort of bond over and talk about, but Rachel didn't have much in common with their career-focused parent. She saw him maybe once a month and at holidays and rarely invited him to dinner.

"I'm just saying that even rock stars make mistakes," she said. She kept her gaze on the plants in front of her, but a hint of tension rested in her shoulders and the curve of her spine.

"Do you know something about Lily that I don't know?" Rachel worked part-time as a substitute teacher and a tutor, and Lily had been part of a study group she'd been running at the time. Although they hadn't talked much about Lily's disappearance, Mack was sure their father would have asked her what she knew.

"I wouldn't say that exactly." Rachel got to her feet and took her time peeling off the muddy gardening gloves. "Lily was a troubled girl—pretty much everyone knew that, but I don't think she'd run away."

"She ran away from home three times before." He'd read the file, and he knew the history. He didn't need to go researching a case that was already closed.

If that was so, why was he here? Asking Rachel about a girl who Mack agreed had run away from home? Just proving his father was right, he told himself. That was all.

"Yeah, I know, but she was younger when she ran away those other times," Rachel said. "That year she disappeared, Lily was starting to get back on track. She was bringing her grades up and talking about maybe going to college."

"Yet she was hanging out with those kids who did drugs and still arguing with her mother all the time. Plus, she had that breakup and was undoubtedly upset about that. I don't think she was as on track as you think." Rachel was the optimist in the family, but Mack had seen enough in his job to know better. The reality very rarely matched the perception that other people had.

"Maybe not." A long, dark sedan swung into the driveway. Rachel's husband got out of the car, briefcase in hand, and his suit jacket over his arm. He gave his wife a friendly smile. "Ted's home. Time for tacos."

Mack grinned. "Like I said, sis, it's always time for tacos."

Chapter Three

Kate had been through the thin folder at least a dozen times. She'd read every document, noted all the possible clues and tried to puzzle out the pieces that had been redacted. One witness's name had been blacked out by the police department, even though the witness testimony didn't seem to be anything controversial. From what Kate could piece together, the witness knew Lily, either as a neighbor or a classmate.

There was a list of other witness statements that had been taken, but no transcripts were in the folder, and a very short statement from Ashley, Lily's best friend. Why was that information left out? Or had the witnesses said so little that the detectives didn't think it warranted a typed sheet of paper?

Kate sighed and unfolded herself from the couch. Her legs ached from sitting in one place for so long, and as she bent to stretch, Harley nosed at her leg, clearly eager for a walk. "Okay, buddy, give me a second."

He gave her a happy bark, then dashed over to where his leash hung from a hook on the wall. "I guess you don't want to wait any longer. It's probably way past time I stretched my legs too." She clipped the leash on to the dog's collar and gave his ears a rub. His tail thumped against her leg.

Just as she pulled open the door, Jenn was walking up the stairs, her arms full of groceries and a stack of letters that dangled from between two fingers. "Grab the mail, will you? I'm about to drop it."

Kate took the envelopes and two of the shopping bags from Jenn and helped her carry everything into the kitchen. "Hey, thanks for stopping at the grocery store. I forgot."

"I know you, and when you get deep into a case, you forget to eat." Jenn pulled a box out of one of the sacks. "So, I got you some Pop-Tarts. They might not be healthy, but they are quick and easy eating when you're stuck at that cardboard box you call a desk."

Kate gave Jenn a hug. "You're the best."

"I grabbed the mail but didn't have a chance to sort it," Jenn said as she unpacked the bags and hurried to stow the food. "If the electric bill is in there, let me know my half for the month when I get home from work."

"Sure, no problem. Hey, I'm going to walk Harley. Want to come along?"

Jenn shook her head. "I'm already late. Next time." She gave her a one-armed hug, then headed out the door.

When Jenn was gone, Kate rifled through the envelopes and stopped when she saw the stamp covering the seal on the back of the envelope. *Piedmont Correctional Institution.*

Kate's breath caught. She peeled open the flap and unfolded the single sheet of paper.

Familiar handwriting filled the lines. Luke's killer had sent her letters before, all of them the same, protesting his innocence and telling her she had it all wrong. He'd asked her to come to the prison to hear his side of the story. Begged her to write back to him. She'd ignored every single letter, and eventually he'd stopped sending them.

Until today.

This time, John David Wheatly didn't bother with a salutation. He'd written only three lines, his handwriting big and full, and even though it was a handful of words, the letter sent a chill down her spine.

You think you know the truth. You've been wrong all this time. Look closer, and you'll see the person you're looking for could be in your backyard right now.

Kate shoved the letter back into the envelope and stuffed it in her pocket. But even out of sight, the words chilled her.

From day one, Wheatly had said he had nothing to do with Luke's death, but he'd never been able to explain why Luke's car was in his yard. There were no fingerprints on the car, no DNA except for Luke's, but also no reason for Luke's car to be mixed among a half-dozen rusting junkers on the dirt lot of that remote cabin high above Soco Gap. Wheatly had a rap sheet as long as her arm, filled with burglaries and assaults, and the prosecutor had put together a case of a robbery gone wrong. The jury had debated less than an hour before sentencing Wheatly to twenty-five years to life.

For the first time since Luke's death, Kate wondered if maybe she had missed something. And if that meant the wrong person was sitting behind bars.

Mack filed his report on the missing stone bunny, along with two reports of vandalism, one car break-in and a suspicious vehicle in someone's driveway. All together, it added up to a lot of what he normally saw in the tourist season. In other words, not much more than a bunch of high school and college kids having fun when their parents were busy hiking or shopping.

He pulled out his phone and scrolled through the podcast app. It didn't take much searching to find Kate McAllister's show and see that it had more than a thousand five-star reviews. The trailer for the Lily Ridge case was short, just a couple minutes, all of it implying that the Fordham Police Department hadn't done its job.

He hit Subscribe anyway. Better to know what the enemy was saying—and what she was making the public believe—than to let misinformation build up steam like a runaway train. And, he had to admit as he listened to the first episode of the season, Kate had a nice voice, the kind that seemed both strong and soothing at the same time. Listening to her was oddly familiar and comforting—if he ignored what she said about his father's investigation.

As he headed out of the station, Doc Josephs was coming up the marble stairs. "Detective."

He gave the former coroner a polite nod. "Afternoon. Uh…what are you doing here?"

"Picking up my last paycheck. It's ridiculous that this town would fire me after fifteen years of dedicated service."

Dedicated service? Maybe in the early years, but lately, Josephs had made more mistakes than anyone Mack knew, from forgetting to run tests to hurrying through autopsies and missing critical information. It was past time the department fired him for his ineptness and started looking into the last few cases under Josephs's watch. "Well, good luck to you." Mack started to brush past him.

Josephs stopped him with a hand on his shoulder. "I know pretty much everyone inside that building thinks I'm an idiot, and maybe I am. But I'm not the only one who made a mistake or overlooked something that he shouldn't have."

Irritation boiled inside Mack. Josephs made it sound like all he'd done was forget to cross a t or dot an i. "Those kinds of errors make a big difference when we're trying to find a murderer, Josephs. You're lucky we had the car sitting in Wheatley's yard, or a murderer would be walking free today."

Josephs swallowed those words and waited a beat. "I guess I deserve that, although I will go to my grave saying there was something wrong with the murder of that boy. I never quite put my finger on what it was. You all rushed to judgment and put that Wheatly man in jail—"

"I'm not having this conversation. You know, if my father was still working here, he wouldn't have let you get away with this level of ineptitude. I'm surprised he didn't find a way to have you fired long ago."

Josephs laughed. "Your father? Really? Trust me— that man had more reason to keep me here than to get rid of me."

"What are you saying, Josephs?" The urge to throttle the man until he explained roared through Mack, but he stayed where he was. Violence would accomplish nothing and would only give credence to Josephs's foolishness. The man might have been a great coroner once but now he was nothing but a liability.

"Nothing. I'm not saying anything." The door to the station opened and two patrol officers came outside, chatting about the Dodgers game the night before. Josephs shot them a glance, then stepped away from Mack. "Have a good day, Detective."

Mack debated following Josephs but in the end decided the man wasn't worth his time. The coroner was just spouting off out of frustration or resentment or both.

But he couldn't shake this feeling of missing something. Of some detail he had overlooked. Maybe Kate had gotten in his head after he'd listened to her podcast and made him doubt what he knew—he *knew*—to be true.

His father was a good cop, an even better detective, who had been thorough and meticulous in his work. Mack could only hope to be half as good of an investigator as Dad. There was nothing missing in the file, no screwups. His father had done his job, and Josephs was just trying to shift the blame now that his buddy had retired and wasn't here to stick up for him anymore.

Still, Mack found himself driving past the coffee shop after he left work, instead of taking his usual route home. Even though the shop was closed, he could see a light burning inside and Kate sitting at the counter, sipping coffee while she studied something. She was staring intently at a piece of paper, and he could swear he saw her hand shake as she brought it closer to her face.

He parked in one of the angled spaces. She glanced up when his headlights shone into the shop. Even from here, he could see the confusion on Kate's face. He knocked on the glass door and gestured to her.

She unlocked the door but only opened it a crack. "Can I help you, Detective?"

For a second, he forgot why he had stopped. There was something about the way she had her hair in a messy bun, her face devoid of makeup, wearing jeans and a T-shirt with the shop logo that made his brain sputter. "Uh… I… I thought I'd see if you had any questions on the file."

She considered him for a moment, maybe wondering if he was kidding. "Actually, I do. Would you like to come in and have a cup of coffee?"

"Decaf, if you have it, or I'll never sleep."

Kate tossed him a smile over her shoulder as she led the way into the shop. "I thought cops downed the high-test formula all day long."

"Not the ones who want to sleep at night." He grinned. "I will, however, take one of those scones, if you have any left."

"I don't have any scones, but I do have one slice of chocolate cake with peanut butter frosting."

He patted his stomach. "That sounds like the kind of thing I need to run ten miles to erase."

She laughed. "You and me both. How about we split it?"

"That's an offer I can't refuse. Plus, it's good community building to patronize local shops."

"Win-win." She grinned, then got to work pouring herself a fresh cup of coffee and a steamy cup of decaf for him. The slice of cake sat square in the center of a pale blue plate, flanked by two forks. She stood behind the counter and picked up one fork, while he slid onto the stool opposite her and picked up the other. "You asked if I had any questions, and I do."

For once, skipping the small talk to get straight to work left Mack with a sense of disappointment. Which was insane. He was here to settle some nagging doubts, not to become friends with the one woman who thought he couldn't do his job. "Sure. What can I help you with?"

He'd expected her to ask about some of the police jargon or the codes they used on the reports, but instead, she tugged out the photo of Lily's backpack, sitting on the ground. The purple bag was slightly open, the zipper down just enough to reveal the bulk of the contents. "You're going to think I'm crazy." She scoffed. "Even I think I'm crazy. I shouldn't even ask you this, but…"

"But what?" he prompted.

"See that book right there?" She pointed at the corner of a library book that was peeking up a little higher than the schoolbooks. A few letters of the title could be seen along with the rich green of a forest decorating the cover and spine. "That's Bill Bryson's book *A Walk in the Woods*. It's all about his attempt to hike the Appalachian Trail. I know this because I have seen this book before."

"Okay. So what's your question?"

She lifted her gaze to his, deep green eyes locking on his own. "What is my dead fiancé's book doing in Lily Ridge's backpack?"

Chapter Four

After the words were out of her, the sentence spoken, Kate stared at the picture in her hands, still half hoping it was a mirage, half hoping it was a clue to lead her to finding Lily, which made no sense if Luke was somehow involved—an impossibility because Luke was gone. Luke had already been dead for a month before Lily disappeared. There didn't seem to be any way that their cases could be connected. Except...there was the book.

Everything she thought she knew had been turned upside down when she'd come across this single photo in the file. There were surely thousands, maybe hundreds of thousands, of copies of Bill Bryson's book in print. Maybe a half dozen circulating just through this small town's library.

This edition was like all the others, except for a tiny white circle and the slightest hint of the edges of red letters almost out of the frame. In her heart, she could see that day, hear Luke's laughter when she'd peeled off the label on her banana and stuck it on his thumb. They'd been curled on his couch, just an ordinary end to an ordinary day. The TV had been playing some silly show she barely cared about, and Luke had opened his book to read. It was the kind of comfortable togetherness that she'd dreamed of, the exact kind of marriage she was looking forward to with the two of them reading by the fire while they grew old and more in love by the day. He'd retaliated by putting the sticker on her nose, and just as she'd reached to put it on his cheek, he held up the book like a shield and the sticker had landed in the top right corner.

"Don't," Luke said when she went to peel it off. "Leave it there for now. So I'll think of you every time I open it up when I'm away."

He had taken the book with him when he left on the youth group retreat he had planned in his job as the youth pastor. He had come home for just a day before he went away again for two days, a quick trip to visit his grandmother. Mow her lawn, clean up the patio, drag the fallen limbs from the last storm to the curb. Luke and the book were supposed to be back in plenty of time to peel off the sticker, return the book to the library and spend the rest of their lives together.

Except it hadn't worked out that way at all. None of her dreams had.

She traced the outline of the book. "It was only supposed to be two days."

"I know." Mack's voice was quiet, almost sympathetic.

She jerked her head up, about to ask him how he knew about Luke's trip, all those details about where he was and what had happened. For a second, she thought he'd read her mind or peeked at Luke's file but then she remembered he was a cop, and his father had been the detective assigned to Luke's murder. "Did you work the case too?"

"In a way. It was my dad's case, but he brought me along on some of his witness interviews and kept me in the loop. He knew I wanted to be a detective and this case was the first one I actually got to get somewhat hands-on with. It was pretty cool—" He shut his mouth and his cheeks reddened. "I'm sorry. I didn't mean that the way it sounded. What happened to your fiancé was a terrible tragedy."

"I like puzzles, too, Detective. I get it." She touched his hand, a brief brush of hers against the back of his fingers. "You don't have to apologize."

A moment of something that could have been awkwardness, could have been understanding, stretched between them. Then the detective cleared his throat and took another bite of the cake. He shifted from sympathetic human into stern officer in an instant. "Before we go making any assumptions about that book, Ms. McAllister, I think you should look at the rest of the file. It's been more than a couple years since you lost your fiancé, and I don't mean any disrespect, but memory is a tricky thing and…"

"You think I'm wrong, don't you?" His clear disapproval of her beliefs ignited her temper. Did he think she was stupid?

"You have been wrong before."

His words hung in the shop, cold and stark. And true. Kate swallowed hard. "You have a point. But most of what happened last summer with Elaine's case wasn't on me. It was on the people taking matters into their own hands."

"Encouraged by you and this podcast." His dark eyes met hers and held. Time ticked by on the clock, with the only other sound in the room being the drip of freshly made coffee falling into the pot. "If it wasn't for your involvement, no one would have been here and no one would have gotten hurt. We had that case under control."

"I thought I could make a difference in real time. I mean, she disappeared just a few days before I started the new season, and there was so much information in the media and on social media sites and—"

"And you were wrong. You were convinced we had a serial killer in this town and got the whole area riled up about something that happened almost a year after your fiancé was killed. I had media from three states camped outside my office, wanting to know when we would prosecute Wheatly for a second murder. If you'd bothered to check your facts, Ms. McAllister, you would have known that Wheatly was helping a friend fix his truck at the time that Elaine disappeared."

"You have to admit there were a lot of similarities between the two cases."

"There were only the similarities you wanted to see."

"Her car was found on the Blue Ridge Parkway. It was less than a mile from where Luke and Lily were taken. The killer could live near there. Wheatly's house is right there on Soco Road, so close to the parkway he can hear the trucks going by."

"Elaine had a fifteen-year-old hatchback with a broken fan belt. You push a car like that up a mountain and it's bound to break down, which is what happened to her. Her car dying must have been the last straw after losing her job and her house and custody of her kids. Her death was a suicide, not a murder, and you blew it up into something it wasn't."

She hung her head. "I didn't know all that at the time."

"Exactly. Which is why you shouldn't have been spouting theories and encouraging people to investigate on their own." He went to take a sip of his coffee, changed his mind and pushed the mug away. "Two of your listeners got into a car accident downtown. They almost drove straight through the pharmacy because they thought they saw a witness you were looking for." His face hardened. "I was there when Henry saw that Chevy come barreling through the plate glass window at the drugstore. There were five customers inside. It could have been much worse than it was."

"Insurance covered the damage. And no one got hurt." But even the thought of the pharmacist being hit by a vehicle, or of anything that Kate said leading to such a tragedy, made her panic. When she was in her office in the dark talking into the mic, she didn't think about the people on the other end, the audience who might take her information as an invitation to intervene. "But my listeners found Elaine's friend, who told me she had been deeply depressed for some time and struggling with her drinking problem, which corroborated your theory. In a way, they solved the case, Det—"

"Henry took two months off from work. He says he still shakes when he's in the front of the store. There is a toll for what you do, Ms. McAllister, and I don't think you care about the price."

She bristled. He had no idea what she had been through or how much she cared about every single life and every single person in this town. "What about the people who have died? Whose cases I have helped solve?"

"Case, *singular*, and again—" he leaned in, making his point "—we had Luke's murderer pinpointed before you came along and confronted Wheatly."

"Five minutes before because someone called in a tip saying that the car was in Wheatly's yard. I was the one who acted on that tip. You guys didn't show up until after I called you and said I was going in to confront him myself." If she hadn't done that, the Fordham Police would have just sat on the information about Luke's car, and Luke's killer could have gotten away. Just like they were twiddling their thumbs with this girl's disappearance. "Lily—"

"Is a runaway. The last thing this town needs is

hundreds of curious armchair detectives running around with spyglasses and tape recorders thinking they are going to find Jimmy Hoffa's body." He nodded toward the folder. "And now you have the information you asked for. In exchange, I'll ask one favor of you."

She scooped up the papers and stuffed them back in the folder. As much as she wanted to lash out at him, he had done what she'd asked and brought her the case file. She should try to be grateful for that instead of angry at his accusations. "What's that?"

"Drop this investigation. Stop running the podcast. You have a business right here that is doing pretty well, a business that is boosted by tourism numbers, am I right? Concentrate on bringing people to town for the amenities we have to offer, not fabricated crimes that never even happened in Fordham."

She had a sharp and ready retort—words so harsh she would surely regret them later—but before she could speak, he tossed a few bills on the counter and walked out the door, forcing Kate to table everything that had just happened, and stuff her frustration deep down inside. She poured herself a coffee and decided she would figure it out later.

Either way, she would definitely deal with this.

She sat down again at the counter to finish going through the folder in detail. It was lean, which meant the amount of investigation had been minimal. There was an initial missing person's report, a scant interview with Lily's parents, along with a few photos of the car and her backpack. At the back of the folder

Kate found a phone call statement with a woman in Florida who'd called in to report a sighting of Lily in Panama City Beach, which apparently was enough to convince the elder Snyder that she had run away from home. Case closed.

Despite the detective's assurances that the Fordham Police Department was *on it*, Kate had personal experience with seeing how they fumbled investigations or flat out ignored them. The disappearance of Elaine Reynolds had been just as underinvestigated as Luke's case and Lily's. It was only because Kate had either called or shown up in Snyder's office every single day for weeks after Luke died, demanding answers and updates, that things moved forward at all. Even then, the elder Snyder had dragged his feet so much in arresting Wheatly that Kate had taken matters into her own hands.

Sure, she had been wrong about Elaine, but everyone made mistakes. It wasn't like her errors were intentional. It was all part of the effort to get to the truth.

Yet a cloud of guilt hung over her shoulders. What happened with that accident at the drugstore could, indeed, have been much worse. As much as she wanted to get to the truth, she also didn't want anyone else to be collateral damage. She carried more than enough guilt already.

Jenn was just pulling into the driveway of their little apartment home as Kate was getting home. The sun was not quite ready to set, but Kate could already feel the exhaustion of the day in her bones. All she wanted to do was curl up in her bed and sleep for days, but there was a folder of information that she was going to continue to scour and analyze.

Look closer, and you'll see the person you're looking for could be in your backyard right now.

Wheatly's chilling words haunted Kate's thoughts. Was there another killer on the loose? Was he telling the truth? Or was it just some ploy to mess with her mind?

"How was work?" Kate asked as she put her bag and keys on the end table and forced herself to think about anything other than John David Wheatly. Harley wriggled his way between the two girls, as happy to see one as he was to see the other. Kate scratched behind his ears, and the dog pressed his body against her thigh.

"Work was busy as usual. Plus, Miriam Leonard was in. Again. Third time this week." Jenn rolled her eyes.

Miriam Leonard owned five cats, each of them a rescue, that she spoiled rotten. They were mischievous animals, all young and adventurous, which made for a challenge every time they came into the veterinarian's office. "Let me guess." Kate thought a second. "BooBoo was crying in his cage so she let him out again."

Jenn nodded. "Right in front of a Doberman puppy who wanted to play. The two of them ran through the office, knocking over the chairs and a potted plant, until BooBoo darted through the swinging door when we came out to see what all the commotion was. BooBoo wedged himself into the space at the top of the cabinets. Took us a solid half hour to get him to come out." Jenn dumped her messenger bag in the chair by the front door and let out a long sigh. "I need a month-long spa retreat."

Kate laughed. "I can't give you that, but I can give you one dog walk around the neighborhood."

"Hmm. Not quite the same, but the company is great, so I'll take it." Jenn grinned, then grabbed Kate's jacket off the hook by the door and handed it over.

After clipping Harley's leash on his collar, Kate shrugged into the lightweight jacket and the two of them headed out into a misty but warm early evening. The fresh, sweet scent of the mountains hung in the air, a familiar friend that settled into her bones with a sigh.

"So," Jenn said as they ambled down the driveway, with Harley tugging Kate's arm and urging them to hurry up. "I can tell from the look on your face that something happened today. Good or bad?"

Kate brushed past the shrubs that edged the wooded path behind their house. The rich earth on the path was damp and musty, and a dark, emerald hush fell over everything else. The path opened up and Jenn fell into step beside her. "Neither. More… intriguing."

She could have told Jenn about Wheatly's letter but already knew that would set Jenn off on a whole lecture about staying safe and not engaging with the convicted murderer. Instead, Kate tugged her phone out of her back pocket and opened the pictures app. She'd snapped a picture of the crime scene photo earlier today and studied it at least a hundred times since then, hoping she was wrong as much as she hoped she was right. Now she enlarged the photo to show the corner of the book and top half of the bag, then handed the phone to Jenn. "That's Lily's backpack."

Jenn nodded. Even though she wasn't part of the podcast, she'd listened to Kate often enough to be familiar with the facts. "They found that on the road beside the car, right?"

"Yup. It was filled with the usual teenage stuff— schoolbooks, a friendship bracelet, a few overdue homework assignments and half a granola bar. But there was also this." She pointed at the dog-eared corner of *A Walk in the Woods*.

"A library book?"

"Not just any library book. *Luke's* book."

Jenn stared at the picture for a moment longer, her brows knitted in confusion, then handed the phone back. "That's crazy, Kate. I mean, no offense, because you know I have a hundred percent supported you looking into these cases—even if I feel you put too many hours into it—but there's no connection between Luke and Lily. How would he have even known her?"

"He was the youth pastor at Mountainside Church. He met dozens of teenagers there. Maybe even Lily." Just because Kate didn't remember Luke mentioning Lily didn't mean he hadn't worked with her or seen her in his group. He'd been working a full-time job at the tourist center in downtown Fordham and serving as the youth pastor, while Kate had been busy running the coffee shop. Their time together then had been limited, mostly quick catch-ups about their days. The two of them had been so sure that there would be plenty of time to talk after they got married and were living together.

Jenn stopped walking. Kate paused while Harley explored the shrubs beside them. "But Luke died before Lily disappeared," Jenn said. "How did she end up with his library book? If it even is his."

"It is. See that?" Kate pointed at the curve of the white sticker, and the memory flooded her all over again in a rush of emotion. "That's from a banana. I know this sounds crazy, but I remember accidentally putting that on his book. It was the day before he left on the youth group retreat, just a few days before he…"

Jenn didn't say anything. Instead, she drew Kate into a long, tight hug, until the heavy lump of grief and regret dissolved. Harley tugged at his leash, his happy tail brushing against Kate's leg, and they began moving again. Kate whispered a silent thank-you to God for such an understanding and supportive best friend who knew just the right thing to do.

Jenn took Harley's leash, which gave him free rein of the east side of the trail. "Okay, so if that's true, and if you say it is, then I believe you. How can you make sure it is the same book? I mean, the picture only shows a corner. That's not a lot to go on."

"I need to see the evidence in person. Which unfortunately means working with Mack Snyder, who I'm pretty sure hates me because of what happened last summer." She told Jenn about the conversation she'd had with the detective earlier. "He asked me to drop this case and stop putting my nose into things the Fordham Police Department has under control."

"He does realize you don't control anything other people do, right? That accident was not your fault."

Kate shrugged. "Doesn't matter. He thinks I'm just a nuisance that he has to tolerate because of the FOIA request. Now that he's done his part and given me the file, I doubt I can get him to cooperate with me or convince him that Lily's disappearance is foul play. His father closed the case, and Mack Snyder seems reluctant to challenge anything when it comes to what his father may or may not have done while he was a cop."

The girls kept walking until they emerged into a big field. The sun was just starting to dip behind the mountains. In a few minutes, the sunset would be stunning, like every sunset she'd ever seen in this valley.

Jenn gave her a one-armed hug. "Then do what you do best, Katie, and find some evidence even Mr. Uptight Detective can't ignore."

Chapter Five

Another long week where it seemed like all Mack was doing was treading water in mud finally came to a close. Mack walked out of the station a little after seven on a Friday night. The burglary at the hardware store had been solved, attributed to a teenager with a drug problem. It was sad to see how much of the crime in their little town could be traced back to drugs.

Mack sighed, unclipped his gun from his belt, made sure it was unloaded and the safety was on then set it inside the handprint-lock gun box he'd bought several years ago and set by his front door. From the time he was a little boy, his father had drummed into him the importance of gun safety. There'd been endless lessons about using the safety, cleaning the mechanisms and keeping the weapon locked up the minute the day was over. Mack's father had been what they called a cop's cop—blue through and through and dead serious about his job. Those values had rubbed off on his only son and permeated almost every decision Mack made on the job.

In fact, Mack tried twice as hard to be responsible and thorough, if only to live up to his father's reputation and one day hear his father say, *Good job, son.* Those words had never been spoken by James Snyder, but some fairy-tale side of Mack still longed to hear them.

Mack set his heavy belt beside the metal box, then kicked off his shoes before wandering into the kitchen to find something to eat. His fridge was bare, save for a Styrofoam box of leftovers he didn't recognize and a few condiments with questionable expiration dates. The cabinets were no better. A few cans of soup, a couple cans of green beans and a box of crackers that had long ago gone stale.

The thought of the scone he'd had this morning made his stomach rumble. He should have bought a dozen of them while he was there—not just because he was hungry but because he could still indulge in one of his favorite treats and not have to see that annoying, stubborn Kate McAllister.

She also happened to be insanely beautiful, but that had nothing to do with why he was regretting storming out of the coffee shop today. Kate had been wrong—wrong about the book, wrong about the investigation and wrong to insinuate that Mack's father had done a subpar job. James Snyder might have been a terrible husband and a passable father, but when it came to the police force, he made excellence a daily choice, and all Mack could do was hope to be half as good as that.

With another heavy sigh, Mack put his shoes back on, grabbed his keys and headed out into the early evening. There was only one real grocery store in Fordham, a mom-and-pop store that had survived the nearby invasion of the chains. He preferred to frequent the smaller store, partly because it had been the store he remembered going to as a kid and partly to support the locals who worked so hard to keep it running, especially during the off-season. Mack parked in the lot and headed inside the air-conditioned space. The store was mostly empty, the majority of people at home with their families.

Once upon a time Mack had thought that would be his life trajectory too. He'd graduate from the academy, start working for the police department, fall in love, get married and have some kids. From the time he could understand what arguments were, he had been bound and determined to be a different kind of spouse and father.

But that special woman had yet to come along. He'd dated several women over the years, but none of them had been the kind that haunted his every thought. Maybe he'd been too driven, too wrapped up in his job and trying to impress his father, to leave any room in his mind and heart for someone else.

Either way, all that meant he was picking out a frozen dinner for himself again. Not the healthiest of meals, but for a man who couldn't cook or keep his fridge stocked, it was pretty much the best option.

Mack bypassed the fresh vegetables, then the meat aisle, because a man like him with cooking skills that ranged from opening a can to pushing a button had no business trying to assemble something from scratch, then turned left and down the frozen meals aisle.

Almost as soon as he made the pivot, he saw Grace Ridge. Lily's mother seemed to have aged ten years in the last three. Her once vibrant red hair had become a dull copper with strands of gray, and she had a shuffle to her step that hadn't been there before. A heavy, uncomfortable blanket of sadness hung on her shoulders.

Mack couldn't help but feel sympathy for her. Losing a child, no matter how it happened or where that child was, held a pain no one could quantify. He'd seen that firsthand years ago when a childhood friend had been killed in a car accident, and Mack knew the helpless desperation left in the family's wake. He wondered if Lily had ever reached out after she ran away or if she had left her family in the dark out of bitterness or shame.

He was tempted to go the opposite direction and avoid running into Grace. He had no answers for her, nothing to give her except another *I'm sorry.*

She looked up just then, catching his eye. The two of them hesitated on either end of the aisle before Grace made the first move toward him. "Good evening, Detective."

"Evening, Mrs. Ridge." He shifted his weight, trapped in an uncomfortable pause.

"Where are you on my daughter's case?" she asked. "I haven't heard anything in months."

"Ma'am, we will always be looking for answers." Face-to-face, he couldn't quite bring himself to say, *The case is closed. She'll come home if she wants to.*

"Doesn't seem to me you're looking for anything. Especially my daughter. You said you had a credible witness who saw her in Florida, but I think that person was wrong. My daughter would never run away."

"Ma'am, most parents think the same thing, until their kids do run away. We have pursued every lead we had, and everything points to Florida." Mack wondered if his father had followed up with that witness, just to be doubly sure. He made a mental note to check the file tomorrow. "Perhaps Lily will reach out—"

"She is never going to reach out, Detective! Why can't you understand that?" Grace's voice was sharp and loud, then it broke on the last word, fracturing with a sob, and Mack felt like a jerk all over again. "She's gone. All I'm asking you to do is find her so I can bring her home."

"I assure you, we are continuing to look for answers, Mrs. Ridge." Even as he said the words, he knew they were a lie. Grace had answers—she just didn't like them. "I hope you have a good evening." He moved to pass her when she reached out and grabbed his arm.

"Kate McAllister is bringing attention to my daughter's case. Don't you think that's a good thing?

Maybe it can jog someone's memory or bring another clue to light."

"I hope it gives you the answers you're seeking, Mrs. Ridge." He gave her a nod as he took two steps to the left. "Have a good night now."

"She's still out there, Detective. It's your job to find her," Grace called after him. "Please look harder. Please ask more questions, even if the answers are painful."

All he could do was give her another nod and continue on his way. He tossed three frozen meals into his cart without even looking at what they were, then hurried to check out and leave the store. He opened the windows as he drove home, letting in a noisy rush of wind, but it wasn't loud enough to drown out the desperate plea in Grace Ridge's voice.

Proof. She needed proof.

That thought jerked Kate awake at two in the morning. She climbed out of bed, made a cup of English breakfast tea and headed into her office. The chances of her going back to sleep were slim to none, and she was going to need a little caffeine to jumpstart her brain. She booted up her computer and settled in for a long and painful search.

She clicked on the folder titled simply *L* and took a deep breath. A few months after the funeral, she'd combed her phone and computer for pictures of Luke and moved them all into this one folder. Out of sight, but never out of mind. It had been too painful to scroll through her digital albums and stumble across an image of Luke laughing or a silly we-fie of the two of them goofing around. One picture would lead to two would lead to a hundred, trapping Kate in a grief paralysis so deep she didn't leave her bed for days.

Instead of going to the set of photos she needed, Kate started at the beginning of the folder and journeyed down the photographic path of meeting Luke, dating Luke, falling in love with him and then accepting his proposal. There was a group photo of Luke and his friends, along with several of Kate's friends at Lake Junaluska, an impromptu day on the water that had brought the two of them together. Luke had always been on the periphery of her friends group, someone she'd glimpsed but never talked to. This particular day, God had nudged her toward him, and she'd struck up a conversation with the tall, lanky youth pastor as he flipped burgers on a portable grill. As the sun was setting and everyone was packing up to go home, he'd asked her on a date.

She'd been half in love with him before the end of that first night. He'd been so kind, so patient, so sweet. Everything she'd ever looked for and wanted in a man. Where she was driven, he was content. Where she was vocal, he was quiet. They were opposites in nearly every way, but somehow it had just... clicked.

At least most of the time. As the wedding day had drawn nearer, Kate had had moments of doubt that a long-term partnership between two diametrically opposed forces could work. But that was all in the past, a waste of thought, because of course she would have been deliriously happy with Luke, if she'd had that chance to love him forever.

She swiped away the tears on her cheeks and drew in another, shakier breath. The last thirty or so photos comprised the final few weeks of Luke's life. They were the ones she'd avoided for so long. She clicked and there he was, with his big, goofy smile and his messy hair. He was boarding a bus for a youth group getaway and had turned on the step to wave at Kate at the same time she snapped the photo. His face filled the frame, and a sharp pain filled her heart.

She clicked again, and there were the photos he'd sent her from the retreat. There'd been no real reason to save them because she only knew a handful of the teens. The photos had come in one batch from Luke's cloud link, and her computer had downloaded them all. Kate had intended to delete the ones that didn't have Luke in the frame, but then he'd died and…

Well, there were a lot of things she never got around to after that.

The first photo in that collection was of the full group of teenagers, standing in front of the big yellow bus, holding a sign above their heads. *Mountainside Church Fall Youth Retreat! Get Inspired by Nature and Jesus!*

She was about to click to the next photo when something caught her eye. Kate scrolled her mouse, widening the photo and waiting a painstaking second for the computer to refocus the image.

And then she was there, unmistakable and as familiar as a member of Kate's own family. Lily

Ridge's shy smile, shadowed by a ball cap and the sign she was hoisting above her head.

Oh, God. Thank You for nudging me to look here. It was a tie, one that Kate didn't understand, but nevertheless another piece of the puzzle that could eventually unravel Lily's fate.

Kate scrambled to turn on her microphone and start the recorder. Harley nudged the door open, ambled in and settled himself at her feet, but Kate barely noticed. "I have an interesting clue in Lily's disappearance, listeners. Something that could link Lily to my fiancé Luke's murder. I know it sounds crazy, but there is evidence that Luke knew Lily. He was killed just a month before she went missing. Is there a possibility their cases are related?"

She went on to talk about the image of the book she'd seen, then the group photo at the youth retreat. "If you or anyone you know was on the Mountainside Church Youth Retreat that October, reach out to me. Either post in the forums or send me a direct message through the show's page. If you want to be anonymous, that's fine with me. All I want to do is bring Lily home and give her family the answers they need."

There was passion in her voice, the same rushing whisper that Luke had called her "no detours" sound. It meant Kate was going to plow full-speed ahead, regardless of what obstacles or road signs might be in her way.

You have been wrong before.

The detective's words echoed in her head. What

if she was wrong about this connection? What if she got people riled up about something that was just a coincidence? "I'm not saying that Luke's case is definitely connected to Lily's," she said, adding that note of caution to her tone. "I could be running down a rabbit trail that's going to lead nowhere. I'm just musing out loud today. We should wait for more information before anyone—especially me—makes any assumptions. Be safe out there, listeners. Somebody cares about you."

Then she clicked off the microphone and shut down the recording equipment. Tomorrow night she would edit the tape and then drop the episode. Kate rose and picked up her cold tea. At the last second, she reached for her computer mouse and hit Print.

Chapter Six

"That woman doesn't know the meaning of the word *quit*." Mack sighed and got to his feet. He'd been at his desk for less than thirty seconds that Monday morning when the chief came in and told him Kate was at the front desk. Again.

"Just remember. No negative press. It's tourist season, Snyder, and this town can't afford another hit. We don't want the world thinking we've got a serial killer running loose on the streets again."

"Yes, sir." As he headed out to the front desk, an odd twinge of anticipation rose in his chest. Almost like he was looking forward to seeing Kate. Impossible. She was the pesky buzzing fly in his ear all day, every day. No one looked forward to that.

But when he rounded the corner and her wide green eyes met his, there was no doubt that what he felt was the exact opposite of dread. Her long blond hair was up in its usual ponytail, giving her serious face a youthful edge. She had on a bright pink

T-shirt with the coffee shop's logo, a color that only served to deepen the color of her eyes, and the anticipation he'd been feeling warmed into something sweet. "Ms. McAllister. Good morning. How can I help you today?"

She opened her mouth, then shut it again. "Oh, uh, good morning, Detective Snyder." The words stumbled out of her as if his warm greeting had thrown her. Then she seemed to collect herself, even as he swore he saw a flush of pink in her cheeks. She held up the folder she'd been clutching. "I have something I'd like to show you. Do you have a minute?"

A few niceties and already the tension between them had eased a couple degrees. A good start to his Monday, Mack decided. A really good start. "Sure. Let's go in the conference room." He held the door for her and led her down a narrow hallway and then into a tiny office dominated by an oval table and six chairs. Conference room was a generous description for the cramped space. When the entire force of Fordham was in the room, even though they were a small department, the space became standing room only.

"Do you want a cup of coffee?" he asked, reaching for the pot on the warmer.

That brought a smile to her face. "No offense, but I always bring my own." She held up a stainless steel tumbler emblazoned with the shop's name before taking a seat at the table. "I suspect the coffee in the police station isn't as good as what I brew."

"That suspicion is a fact." He set the carafe back

in place without pouring a cup for himself. "Our coffee tastes like wallpaper glue."

She made a face at the dark brown sludge in the pot. "Why don't I pop by later today with a bag of Yirgacheffe roast? It's from Ethiopia, and it's the best roast I have at the shop, as well as a customer favorite."

"That would be great, and much appreciated, believe me. Thank you." He leaned forward and lowered his voice. "Although if this is an effort to butter me up to work with you…"

Her face froze.

"Throwing in a couple scones will work well in your favor." He winked, then caught himself. Since when did he *wink*? And when had he ever been in this good of a mood on a Monday morning?

Relief flooded her features and she answered his smile with one of her own. "Consider it done."

His stomach rumbled at the thought of one of those delicious scones. All memory of how annoying her persistence could be were gone. Warming to a member of the media—a member he had been warned to treat with caution—was treading down a dangerous path because it meant Mack was losing his objectivity.

He drew himself up and cleared his throat. *Focus on the business at hand, not the idea of having a cup of coffee with Kate McAllister.* "You said you wanted to show me something?"

She withdrew a photo from the folder and slid it across the table. Mack sat in the opposite seat and picked up the glossy eight-by-ten. Two dozen or so teenagers were posing in front of a school bus, flanked by a few adults on either end, many of them helping to hold up a sign for Mountainside Church. Mack recognized Luke Winslow's lanky frame right away, as well as several other faces of teens and volunteers, but the photo didn't seem to have any special significance at first glance. "What am I looking at here?"

"That youth group retreat was a few days before Luke died. He's there—" she pointed at her late fiancé "—and Lily Ridge is right there." She tapped on a face in the center of the photo. Mack focused on the young girl's features and recognized the high cheekbones and wide green eyes. He'd seen those same eyes last night when he'd run into Grace Ridge.

As always happened when he was on an investigation, all his senses narrowed to focus on the object before him. He could almost hear the kids laughing and talking, the putter of the bus waiting for them to leave, the warmth of the sun on their faces. Lily looked like every other teenager there, excited about the trip, and not one bit angry or ready to run away.

That didn't mean she hadn't had a big fight with her mother after she got home, or hadn't been devastated by the breakup with her boyfriend. But in that moment, Lily Ridge looked…happy.

"You said there was no way Luke's book could have ended up in Lily's backpack," Kate said, "but here they are, in the same place, a week before he was murdered and a little over a month before she disappears."

"That doesn't mean his death is related to her running away." Although it was an odd coincidence, he had to admit. Two cases, linked by a book? What were the chances of that?

Kate let out a long, heavy sigh. "She didn't run away. She's still out there, and we need to find her to bring her home."

Grace had said much the same thing to him last night. *It's your job to find her. Please look harder. Please ask more questions, even if the answers are painful.* A flicker of guilt squeezed his chest. Had he done all he could do when it came to Lily Ridge?

"Listen," Kate went on, "I know we have our differences of opinion about the Ridge case. But will you just humor me and show me the book you found in her backpack? Because if it is the same as this one…" She tugged a second photo out of the album, this one of Luke sitting on a bench at the campground. Elbows propped on his knees, he was talking to a group of the teenagers, his face animated and bright. And there, beside him on the wooden seat, was a book. Mack recognized the deep green of the cover in an instant.

Mack looked up. "Do you still have the photo of Lily's backpack?"

"Right here." She slid it across the table. "It's the—"

"It bears a resemblance," he cut in as he set the two images side by side. "That doesn't make it the same book." He studied the two pictures for a long time. Kate waited, silent and patient, a departure from her more confrontational attitude with him. The silence gave Mack a moment to process what he was seeing. He liked to do that with a case—sit back, let the information marinate a bit, before he reacted or moved on a hunch. The more he stared at the pictures, the more he knew he was going to make a decision that was definitely going to get him in trouble. "Let's go take a look at the evidence box."

She sprang out of her seat. "Really? I didn't think you'd agree so easily."

"On one condition." He held up a hand. "That you don't talk about anything you see in the evidence box on your podcast."

"Detective, this is an investigation. You can't tie my hands like that." She drew in a breath and seemed to calm her immediate rush of irritation. "But I can see how exposing too much could hurt your chances of catching the person who took Lily. How about we take a look at the evidence box and then we discuss whether sharing any of that information on my show could compromise the investigation?"

He arched a brow. "Are you actually trying to work with me instead of against me?"

She raised her chin and met his gaze. "I'm not an unreasonable person, Detective. And neither, I suspect, are you."

There was something about the way she was looking at him that made him think about sitting down with her at the end of the day and enjoying one of those promised cups of coffee, or maybe something other than a prepackaged meal. She seemed the type of woman who would make a casserole while he cleaned up, the two of them lingering in the kitchen long after the food was put away.

"I'll think about it," was all he said, because he didn't know what else to say. Where were all these thoughts of domestication and dating coming from? *Back to business*, he reminded himself. *Work is your priority, not a woman.* "Wait here, please. I'll go get the box and come back."

The whole way to the evidence room, Mack told himself he was insane. The case was closed. They had an eyewitness, someone who had seen Lily in Florida. Except Mack had looked in the file first thing today, and there was no follow-up interview with the witness. Mack had a name—Anne Smith—that was so common, it would be almost impossible to track her down. There was no return phone number or address, none of the usual details gathered in a witness report. Had his father decided Lily's fate after a single phone call from a stranger? No. James Snyder would never do that.

But Mack was also not going to leave any other stones unturned, which was why he was heading for the evidence room. If the chief found out that Mack was indulging the podcast's requests, there'd be a price to pay, that was for sure. Maybe even a disciplinary action. The hard work Mack had done to live up to the untarnished reputation of his father could all be undone in the blink of an eye—or the opening of a box. And then Mack would go right back to being the lesser son of the hero detective.

The images of the book gnawed at him though. The two paperbacks looked almost identical, at least from the outside and the tiny square he'd seen in the photo Kate had shown him. It was a fluke, he told himself.

Except Mack Snyder didn't believe in flukes. His mother called things like that *the hand of God making an appearance*. If that was so, then what message was God trying to send?

There was an easy way to settle this whole thing once and for all, and it was found buried in a box. Once he showed Kate the book, she'd realize she was wrong. But the closer Mack got to the evidence room the more he suspected Kate was a hundred percent right.

He signed the bankers' box containing everything related to Lily Ridge's disappearance out of the evidence room, grabbed a pair of gloves then headed back down the hall. The chief was in his office, yelling into the phone. He glanced up as Mack passed and raised a brow in question but didn't disconnect his call. There would be questions asked and answers to give later, Mack knew.

His step faltered. All his life, he'd worked to live up to the impossible reputation of the man who had fathered him. He'd dreamed of being the hero who saved the day or solved the case. What did it say about him that he was questioning work his father had already completed?

And what if he was completely wrong? Would that make him a terrible son? A horrible detective? Destroying his father's decisions was the exact opposite of trying to live up to James Snyder's reputation.

He found Kate pacing the small room when he returned. She stopped walking, let out a long breath and squared her shoulders. "Okay, let's see it."

Mack set the box on the table and the two of them sat in chairs flanking the large cardboard container He took off the lid and peered inside. Everything was neatly arranged, tucked into the box in *Tetris* perfection, something his father had been almost obsessed with. *Order in everything and all things in order,* he'd said more than once.

Amid the few sealed plastic bags, there was an evidence log, a collection of fingerprints they had taken from the outside of the car and the steering wheel and copies of the witness testimonies his father had gathered. Even with the backpack, the box was only half filled.

The first bag was heavy, thick. Lily's backpack, a faded purple with her namesake flower on one corner, sagged in his hands, as if it was unhappy to be left behind. A smaller bag held Lily's car keys, another held an empty soda can, a third contained one of those braided bracelets girls gave to each other. The fifth bag, seated on the bottom of the box, contained a thick book.

Kate gasped. "It *is* his book. Oh my God."

"'*A Walk in the Woods* by Bill Bryson,'" Mack read. The broad furry face of a grizzly bear peeked

After She Vanished

over the author's name, almost like he was watching Mack. A deep, lush, green wooded landscape filled the rest of the book's cover. And in the upper right-hand corner, just as in the picture from the crime scene, was a faded but distinctive oval-shaped white sticker that Mack saw every morning when he grabbed a piece of fruit on his way to work.

Even inside the bag, Mack recognized the thick plastic laminate protective cover. He turned the package over and there on the bottom back were the words *Fordham Public Library*, printed in red ink across the laminated surface. "Let me see those pictures again."

She slid them over to him without a word, but he could feel how tense she was, her body coiled and tight. Mack held up the campground picture and stared hard at the book on the bench. "I can't tell for sure if there's a sticker on this one."

"That's because it was dim by the campfire. The photo is a little blurry, but I swear it was there. The day before he left for the retreat, we had the little tussle with the sticker. He came home from the retreat and was here for a day before he hit the road again after his Wednesday night youth group meeting. He never..." She paused. "Never came home again."

He set the photo on the table. He'd hoped for a smoking gun, a definitive sign that she was wrong. What he got was a murky maybe. *A fluke is the hand of God making an appearance.* Well, if that was so, God should have been a little clearer. "There's no proof, Ms. McAllister."

"Kate, please. And there is proof." She pointed at the library stamp on the back of the paperback. "All you have to do is check the library records and see who last checked the book out."

"I'm sure my father did that when he investigated the case. I doubt I'll find anything new."

"If he did, then why isn't that information in the case file? There is no record of Detective Snyder calling the library. I know because I read every word of that case file more than once." She nodded toward his cell. "It'll take you five minutes, Detective. Five minutes, and then you can tell me I'm crazy and to get out of your hair for good."

He considered her for a long moment. One phone call, and he could disprove Kate's theory once and for all. There was no way the murder of Luke Winslow and Lily Ridge's disappearance were connected. None at all.

"I know that the whole thing doesn't make any sense," she said, as if she'd read his mind. "But I've proven to you that my fiancé had a connection with Lily. It's possible he gave her the book at the youth retreat. Luke was that kind of person. He didn't hold on to material things, and he was always lending out his tools and his car and, most of all, his books. I'm sure he thought he'd see Lily again and get the library book back before it was due."

"We have already closed this case," he said. Maybe if he said it enough, she'd let it go. And maybe he would stop wondering if his father had been wrong. Because if his father had been wrong about the Winslow case and the Ridge case, what else was Dad wrong about?

Or was Mack just completely off base and risking his fledgling career for nothing?

One look at Kate McAllister's face and he knew she was never going to drop it. Her green eyes held the same emotions as Grace Ridge's had the other night—hope, despair and entreaty.

"One phone call," he said, and as he pulled on the gloves and took the book out of the evidence bag, he had a feeling he was going to deeply regret what he was about to do.

Chapter Seven

Kate didn't need to hear what the librarian said to Mack. His face went white as he asked the woman on the other end to repeat the information.

"Thank you," he said before he hung up the phone. He took his time tucking the book back into the evidence bag, then pulling off the latex gloves. It didn't matter. She already knew what he was about to tell her, and Kate couldn't decide if she felt relieved or scared that her hunch had been right.

"Luke Winslow withdrew *A Walk in the Woods* two weeks before he was murdered," Mack said. "And never returned it."

"Because he couldn't." She bit her lower lip. "So I'll ask you the same thing I did the other day, Detective. Why is my fiancé's book in Lily's backpack? And what does it have to do with Lily's disappearance?"

"Nothing. Luke Winslow was already dead before Lily disappeared. Lily was in school the day she left town—we have several witnesses who corroborated that fact—so there's no way he could have been involved."

"Maybe the two cases are linked in another way."

He rolled his eyes. "Not this again. Ms. McAllister, not every crime in this town is the work of the same person. You went off on that wild goose chase last summer—"

"We aren't going to have this argument again, are we?" She tapped the plastic envelope holding the book. "Maybe I'm wrong. But either way, you have enough proof to at least start asking some questions, Detective."

"My father investigated this case thoroughly."

"That box seems pretty light for a 'thorough' investigation," she said, using air quotes around the word. "No offense, but your father wasn't doing much about Luke's murder, either. I called him or came down here to see him every single day, and even then I was the one to find the car in Wheatly's yard. I know he's your father, and in this town, he's the revered detective everyone thinks was the best thing since jelly on toast, but even so-called pillars of the community make mistakes."

He bristled at her words, so similar to what Rachel had said. His father might be a lot of things but a sloppy detective wasn't one of them. "You don't know my father."

She covered his hand with her own. Her touch was light, but warm and…nice. And confusing the whole issue. "No, I don't. Not really. I could be totally incorrect about him. And I'm sorry, I truly don't mean any disrespect toward your father. I'm just saying that people make mistakes. They get overwhelmed. They go through stuff in their personal lives. If he overlooked the library book, what else could he have missed?"

Mack clearly didn't have an answer to that. Instead, he got to his feet, returned the materials to the evidence box and closed the lid. "I have to get back to work. I'll take your words under advisement and be in touch in a few days."

She propped a fist on her hip and studied him. "Why do you do that?"

"Do what?"

"Go all 'cop' on me. You get distant and almost clinical in the way you talk to me whenever I bring up the possibility that your father was wrong."

"You don't know my father," he said again. "I do."

"Well, Detective," she said as she picked up her folder and held it to her chest, "maybe it's time you talked to the source himself."

She glanced at her watch. "I have to get back to the coffee shop. It starts getting busy again at nine, and that's too much for Jeremy to handle on his own. I'll drop off the coffee beans on my way home."

"Thank you. I'll call you if there are any developments."

"Why don't we meet for dinner instead?" The words were out of her mouth before she could think about the wisdom of what she'd just said, or why she was inviting a man who couldn't stand her out on something that sounded suspiciously like a date. "The Blue Ridge Barbecue at six?"

He blinked. For a second, she was afraid she'd offended him or scared him off. "I haven't eaten there in a long time. I tend to work too much and heat up a microwave meal when I get home." He shook his head. "Sorry. I didn't mean to get personal."

She smiled. "This world would be a lot kinder, I think, if people got more personal. And for the record, my dinner of choice is usually a peanut-butter-and-jelly sandwich. I think we both could use a normal meal."

"Good point, Kate." A slow smile spread across his face. "I will see you at six."

She walked out of the police department, a confused tumble of thoughts in her head. Every time her mind tried to circle around the book and what meaning it had when it came to Lily's disappearance, the image of Mack Snyder's smile came back, along with the merest whisper of excitement about seeing him again.

Chief Reynolds came over to Mack's desk a half hour later. Mack looked up from the search he was running and put up his hands. So far, there was no record of an Anne Smith living in Panama City Beach in the last three years, and nothing in the case notes that could lead Mack to the caller who'd reported a sighting of Lily. "Before you say anything, I'm just chasing down a couple leads that are probably nothing. Once I do that, Kate McAllister will see that she's wrong about Lily Ridge's disappearance."

"What kind of leads?"

Mack explained about the book and the sticker, then told his chief about the witness who had disappeared into thin air. "But it's all a coincidence, nothing more."

"An awfully rare coincidence, don't you think? And I'm not happy that there aren't any details on that witness. I didn't know your father never followed up with her, or if he did, he didn't put it in the case notes." The chief's brows knitted and he stared out the window for a moment. "Go ahead and run with it, Snyder."

"Really? But I thought you don't want me working on this case."

"There's a reason you listened to that McAllister woman and showed her the book. Your father had great instincts. I can't tell you how many times I'd follow him along on what I thought was a fool's errand, only for him to be proved right. You're a Snyder, and if you feel like there might be something to it, then I say chase it down."

The comparison to his father filled Mack with a sense of pride. He'd worked hard to be seen as a good cop, like his dad had been, and for his boss to notice meant a lot. Didn't mean his father would ever see his son as anything of merit, but it was a step in the right direction. "Yes, sir. Will do."

He headed out of the station for the day with a list of stops on his agenda. As he talked to Eugenia Whitcomb about her missing wallet, he thought about the Ridge case. When he stopped at Ned's Sky-view Diner to take a report on an employee who'd pocketed the cash in the register, Mack's mind wandered to Kate. He spent most of the afternoon doing interviews and writing reports, but always in the back of his mind, Kate and the Ridge case lingered.

On his way home, he took a left instead of his usual right. Three miles later, he pulled in front of his father's two-story log home, nestled into a hill-side that looked up to a trio of mountain ridges. For more than fifteen years, his father had lived here and done a pretty extensive renovation of the older home. Like everything else about James Snyder, the house was worthy of a photo spread in *Architectural Digest*.

Mack parked on the gravel driveway. His father came around from the back of the house at the sound of the car. "What brings you by?" he said as Mack got out of the sedan.

"Wanted to talk about an old case with you."

"Here for some pointers from your old man? I knew that would happen. Getting your feet wet on the job and wanting some advice, I'm sure. I'll put on some coffee." Dad waved at Mack to follow him up the stairs and into the house. The elder Snyder was four inches taller than Mack, and about twenty pounds heavier since his retirement. But he still had the same commanding presence with his stern face and deep voice.

Mack took a seat at the kitchen table, setting the

Ridge file in front of him. His father started the coffee maker. "What case are you interested in?" he asked.

"Lily Ridge."

It seemed as if his father stilled for a second, but the moment was so short, Mack was sure he imagined it. "Really? That case has been closed for two years. Girl's a runaway. What are you going to waste your time with that for?"

Mack bristled at the implication that what he was doing was useless. To his father, nothing but James Snyder's way was the right way. Maybe it was because Rachel had been the youngest, and the child who could do no wrong, but Mack had been struggling all his life to prove himself to his father. To be good enough at Little League, at football, at debate team, at police work, for Dad to finally give his only son a pat on the back. Everywhere he went, he was referred to as James Snyder's son, like he was a shadow, not a person in his own right. Heck, even in his own family, Mack felt like a shadow of his father. "I've been over the file several times, and nothing seems amiss except…"

"Nothing is missing in that file. I know. I wrote it myself." His father set two cups of coffee before them and took the opposite seat.

"Except this photo—" Mack withdrew the one of the backpack from the folder "—has an odd detail in it. I'm not sure if you noticed it."

Dad glanced at it and shrugged. "Looks like a teenager's messy backpack to me."

"This book—" Mack tapped on the corner of *A*

Walk in the Woods that was peeking out of Lily's canvas bag "—belongs to Luke Winslow."

His father didn't look up. Every muscle in his body tensed and he bent down, studying the photo even closer. "That's impossible."

"It is and yet…" Mack shrugged. "I checked the book myself. It's a library edition, and when I called the library, they said Luke was the last one to check it out. I would have doubted the connection but Kate McAllister—"

"That woman is nothing but a menace. Don't believe a word she says." His father shook his head and picked up his coffee. "When are you going to learn? The media isn't there to help you, Mack. They're there to point out your mistakes. All you're going to do is bring shame on the Snyder name by affiliating yourself with that woman. She thinks we're all inept, and I will not allow you to tarnish my reputation right alongside yours."

Mack swallowed the first response he had, and the second. Arguing with his father about the Snyder family name—and Mack's damage to it—would only make the situation worse. "Kate McAllister has proof that Luke had the book in his possession shortly before he was killed."

"That's impossible," he said again. His father pushed the photo away so hard it skittered across the table and fell down behind one of the chairs. Dad got to his feet while Mack retrieved the glossy image. "I have work to do in the yard. I don't have time to discuss a case that's been closed for years. If you read the case file, you'll see there's a witness—"

"Who saw her in Panama City a month after she disappeared. Yes, I saw that report. But there was no follow-up, no way to contact the witness again later and verify her story. That's a big detail to miss, Dad. Kate and I—"

"That woman wouldn't know the difference between a clue and a breadcrumb." His father scowled. "This is a pointless conversation. You've been a detective for, what, five minutes? I know you mean well, Mack, but I've got three decades of experience, and I'm telling you, that girl ran away."

"Kate McAllister—"

"Is nothing but an annoyance, as I said. That woman was on my case every single day after the Winslow kid died. She acted like I wasn't doing anything. You know she was about to confront Wheatly herself when we got there? You know what that is? That's sheer stupidity, and a need for some kind of journalism prize. Maybe she's trying to get rich on YouTube. I don't know. What I do know is that you're wasting your time by talking to her, and you're making yourself look like an idiot in the process. I will not have my son disgracing all of us." He dumped the rest of his coffee down the drain, then braced his hands on the sink. He seemed to visibly release the tension in his shoulders, and when he spoke again, his voice was calm and soft. "Son, do you think I was a good cop?"

His father never betrayed vulnerability. Never

acted weak. The question hit Mack hard in the chest. "Dad, you were the best. They practically have a trophy wall dedicated to you down at the station."

"Then why don't you trust me when I tell you that case is closed?"

"Dad, I'm not trying to disrespect your work. I'm just saying that even the best detectives can miss a thing or two." Mack saw his father wince at the last words, and he wished he could take them back.

"I built my reputation on following the leads, Mack, and on doing good police work. Don't go undoing all that with a wild goose chase." His father's steely gaze met Mack's. "Do not disrespect me or this family by dragging the past through the mud. You want to make me proud of what you do on the force? Go solve a case that actually needs to be solved. Until then, don't waste my time."

Kate turned off the mic, then stretched her arms above her head as she worked some kinks out of her back. She'd recorded a short episode after she got home from work, just enough to get some content out for this week. There wasn't much new information to report, not while she was still trying to figure out the connection with the book and Lily, so she did a recap of the day Lily disappeared, taking her listeners from Lily's last day at school to stopping at work to pick up her paycheck. Two hours later, her car was found on Soco Gap, and her backpack a few feet away.

The clock on Kate's desk showed that it was just

after five. She still needed to get ready and drive over to the Blue Ridge Barbecue, so she opted to quit for the night. Just as Kate started to turn everything off, her cell rang. A number she didn't recognize, with a North Carolina exchange, popped up on the screen. "Hello?"

A long pause, so long Kate considered hanging up. Then a tentative, "Is this the lady from the podcast?"

"Yes. I'm Kate McAllister." She softened her tone, waited a beat. "And who am I speaking to?"

"This is Ashley."

Kate froze. For weeks, she'd been trying to get ahold of Lily's best friend from high school. The girl had moved out of Fordham and, according to her mother, was working and living in Asheville after following her boyfriend there. But every number Kate tried and every email she sent had been a dead end. Even Ashley's mother had stopped responding. "Did you get my messages?"

"I... I changed my phone number after this started because, like, so many people were trying to get with me and get answers, and I just... I can't."

"I totally understand that, Ashley. I'm sure it's been so tough. You lost a friend, and then you were thrown into the middle of this investigation." While she was talking, Kate scrambled to turn on the recorder, connect it to her phone, and start the tape. In a one-party consent state, Kate didn't need to ask Ashley, who also lived in the state, if she could record their conversation. And, she suspected, if she said anything about that right now, it would spook the girl. Later, there would be an opportunity to ask her permission. Kate wasn't one of those reporters who hid in the bushes and ambushed people. If Ashley said no to using the recording, Kate would honor her wishes.

"Some people are saying she ran away. Some are saying she committed suicide." Ashley sniffled and her voice choked. "Lily would never do those things. She wasn't like that."

"I know. That's why I'm doing the podcast. I want people to keep looking for her."

"Do you..." Ashley paused. "Do you think she's still alive?"

Kate hesitated. Whatever answer she gave this hopeful girl would be, at best, an educated guess. At worst, a hurtful reality. She had gone too far last summer and got the public riled up too much. This time, she vowed to be more cautious and think through what she put on the air so that no one else got hurt. "I think God gives us hope and the knowledge that no matter what happens, He always has us in the palm of His hand."

There was a long moment of silence. If it wasn't for the sound of passing cars on the other end, Kate would think Ashley had disconnected. "She wasn't going anywhere that day, you know."

Kate fumbled for a notebook and a pen. "Then why do you think she was in Soco Gap?"

"She told me that some guy had scared her. He came into her work a few times and he was all creepy and stuff, and it scared her."

Kate wrote *creepy guy, check with the Skyview Diner* on her notepad. "Did she know who it was?"

"I don't think so. She would have told me if she did. We were like besties. We have been all our lives and...and...we were supposed to always be best friends." And then Ashley started to cry, a soft heartbroken sound that made Kate wish she could reach through the phone line and hug the young woman tight.

"What about Alex? Lily's mom said they had broken up before she went missing."

"They did. But it wasn't like Lily was all upset about it. They were always more like friends than boyfriend and girlfriend. Alex wasn't anyone who would hurt her, and Lily didn't really want to date anyone else. Almost all the boys at Fordham High were stupid anyway."

Kate circled the words she'd written a moment ago on the pad. "Did she say anything else about this creepy guy? Did she see him anywhere other than the Skyview Diner?"

Ashley thought for a minute. "She did say something about thinking she was being followed one night. But that was like a week before everything happened."

Kate wrote down *one week earlier*. This was new information. If the police had known about this mystery stalker, there was no mention of it in the file. Who could it be? "Did you tell the police about this guy?"

"Yup. But the guy I talked to, Detective..."

"Snyder?" Kate finished for her.

"Yeah, the older one. He, like, didn't seem to care. He kinda rushed me off the phone and didn't even ask me to come in and do one of those statement things. Aren't they supposed to do that? Like, I see it on TV all the time."

"The police department typically takes a written statement from a witness. And you're right, he didn't have one from you. The case file only has some notes he made when he talked to you on the phone. Maybe they just didn't find what you told them very relevant." Except a creepy guy who might have followed Lily home couldn't have been more relevant. Why would Snyder ignore Ashley's testimony?

Kate's gaze strayed to the folder, and the image of Luke's book in Lily's backpack. "Ashley, did you go on the youth group retreat? The one that Pastor Luke had before Lily disappeared?"

"Uh, yeah. Why?"

"I found Luke's book in Lily's backpack. Do you have any idea how it ended up there?"

There was a pause, and in the background, Kate could hear someone calling to Ashley. She shouted back that she'd be done in a minute before she returned to the conversation. "Lily was, like, kind of depressed on the retreat. Like, her mom and she didn't get along well at all, and she was really upset. Not, like, so upset that she'd run away. You gotta know that."

"I do. I believe you."

"But something else was bothering her on the retreat. When I asked her about it, she said I wouldn't understand. We kinda had a little fight about it, and I feel really bad. I wish…" Ashley let out a long sigh. "Anyway, Pastor Luke talked to her a lot that weekend when he saw she was upset. He was really good that way, you know, talking to us like we weren't little kids or anything. He said something to Lily about how nature made him feel peaceful or something when he was stressed and stuff." Ashley paused. "Wait. Didn't Pastor Luke die, like, near where Lily went missing?"

"Very close to the same spot, yes."

"That's super weird, right?"

"It is a strange coincidence. But I don't know what kind of connection there could be other than the book. Pastor Luke had already died when Lily disappeared." Kate was wishing that Ashley could just fill in the blanks, solve the puzzle and bring everyone answers. But it was clear that the young girl knew less than Kate did.

"I like what you're doing," Ashley said, "you know, with the podcast?"

"Thank you. I'm just trying to do my part to help bring Lily home."

"I hope you find her. We all hope you do." Ashley started crying again, and Kate gave the girl some silence and space before asking her last question.

"What do you want me to know about Lily, Ashley? What can help find her?"

Ashley was quiet for a long, long time. When she spoke again, her voice was soft and filled with longing, grief and so much love. "She loved the color purple and she loved cats. She was the nicest person you could ever meet, but her life wasn't all sunshine, you know? But in the end, Lily loved people more than anyone I know, and if she's gone, it's not because she wanted to leave."

Chapter Eight

Kate closed out the call with Ashley by asking her permission to air the tape and scheduling a second interview with the girl. "I'm nervous about sharing all this on the air," Ashley said, "but if it brings Lily home, it's worth it. It's hard to face the fact that somebody probably hurt her."

"And if we find out who, we can make sure that person never hurts anyone else," Kate said. "You'll be part of that, Ashley. Thank you for being so brave."

After she hung up with Ashley, Kate switched off the recorder, disconnected her phone from the line and stared at the notes she'd written during the call. *Creepy guy.* There was no mention of an investigation into anyone stalking or harassing Lily in the police report; Kate knew that folder inside and out. Was that because Detective James Snyder hadn't asked the questions? Because he didn't want to be bothered, or because he decided Lily was a runaway before any kind of investigation? Either way, Kate would find out why. She tore off the page, stuffed it into the folder with the police report and hurried out of the office.

Her roommate was standing in front of the hall mirror, adjusting her earrings. Jenn had her hair up and was wearing a black pencil skirt and off-the-shoulder coral top that made her dark hair seem almost ebony. Kate debated telling her about Ashley's call, but Jenn was clearly in a hurry and Kate wanted a chance to get Mack's take on what Ashley had said. "Hey, Jenn, can I borrow that blue dress of yours?"

Jenn stopped what she was doing and gave Kate a look of confusion. "A dress? Do you have a big date or something?"

"Well, I have something. I don't know if I'd call it a date." A flush crept up her neck. Was that what this was? A date? Or just a meeting to discuss the case? "I'm, um, meeting that detective on Lily's case at Blue Ridge Barbecue. I sort of asked him to go to dinner."

"You. Asked a man on a date." Jenn didn't even phrase it as a question. She gaped at Kate as if she'd been replaced by a totally different person. "That's a big step out of your comfort zone."

That was true. Kate had always been cautious in who she dated. Not just because she didn't want to get hurt, but because that kind of happy relationship was such a rarity. Her parents had been more like roommates than partners, and until Luke, Kate had never dated anyone who made her hope for a true romance. Luke had been steady and dependable, not exactly a dashing romance hero or anything, but there was something to be said for a man who was a shelter from life's storms.

Mack Snyder? He was the opposite of Luke. He had *presence* and opinions. He was strong and confident, and smart as a whip. He wasn't afraid to confront her or disagree with her, and she had no doubt that dating him would be like walking into a hurricane. But they weren't going on a date, so none of that mattered. Right? "We were talking about dinner, and how neither one of us ever really eats anything healthy, and the next thing I know, I asked if he wanted to go to dinner." Kate shook her head. "Maybe this is a bad idea. I should cancel."

Jenn took both of Kate's hands in her own. "This is a great idea. It's been three years, Kate, and no one is expecting you to keep holding a torch for Luke. You're allowed to move on. I think this something-date is a nice baby step in that direction."

Kate's eyes misted, and she gave Jenn a watery smile. It had been a long time, and although Kate missed Luke, she had gone through her grief and come out the other side. She was ready to move on with her life, at least in her heart. Mentally, she was still as cautious as a baby bird about to leave the nest. She didn't know how she felt about Mack Snyder and wasn't ready to figure that out, nor did she have any intentions of doing that while Lily Ridge was still missing. "Thank you."

"Anytime." Jenn gave her a hug, then turned to

dash down the hall. "I'll go grab the dress. Do you want me to curl your hair too?"

"You're going to be late if you do, so don't worry about it. Besides, this is not a real date so I don't need to get all fancy," Kate said, more to remind herself than Jenn.

Jenn came back with the dress and pressed it into Kate's hands. Then she grabbed her purse, opened the front door, got the stack of mail and handed it to Kate. "Okay. I've got to go or I'll miss my own date. Have a great time, and tell me all about it when you get home!" Then she was gone, leaving Kate altogether too much time to think about what inviting Mack to dinner might mean.

In the end, Kate ended up curling her hair, applying some makeup and wrestling a pair of strappy shoes onto her feet. Jenn's dress was a fit-and-flare style with a modest V-neck and a slight bell in the skirt that bloomed when she turned from side to side, a fun and flirty look that was definitely outside Kate's jeans-and-T-shirt daily uniform. Kate didn't have a whole lot of hairstyling skill—that was Jenn's department—so she just clipped some of her curls back, leaving a few loose tendrils around her face and the rest of the waves trailing down her back. The reflection in the mirror showed a woman who looked vaguely uncomfortable in the dressy clothes, but not half-bad in the put-together department. She told herself it was all part of the baby steps of moving on, not because she thought Mack Snyder was incredibly handsome.

As she headed toward the door, Kate spied the
mail she'd left on the kitchen table. She started flipping through the pile of envelopes, separating the
mail that had arrived for Jenn from her own, before
putting the shared bills on the kitchen table. When
she reached the last envelope, her heart stopped at
the sight of the return address: *Piedmont Correctional Institute.*

A shiver snaked up her spine. A second letter in
the space of a week? Wheatly had never contacted
her that frequently before. Was he trying to scare
her? Harass her?

Her hand shook, and the writing on the front of
the envelope trembled in response. *Don't open it,*
her mind cautioned. *Don't give him the satisfaction.*

But curiosity overpowered her common sense,
and before she could hesitate, she slipped a finger
under the flap, then tore it open in one quick yank.
A single sheet of paper spilled onto the kitchen table,
just like the last sheet and all the ones before that.
Kate lowered herself into a chair and began to read.

John David Wheatly's long, sloped handwriting
leaned far to the right, as if his words were chasing
each other. The letter was short, barely four sen-
tences. Somehow the starkness of the empty space
around the lines chilled her more than if the page
had been crammed with words.

*I am not the one who killed Luke Winslow. I
know you think I'm responsible, but you have put
the wrong man behind bars. Someone else is going*

*to die because you did this. And when they do, I hope
you take comfort in knowing it was your fault.*

He had underlined the last two words several
times, making them pound in her head like a gong-
ing bell. *Your fault, your fault, your fault.*

No. That wasn't true. Wheatly was just trying to
get under her skin, win some sympathy that would
help him with an appeal or somehow get evidence of
a mistrial or something. Luke's car had been found
in Wheatly's yard. There might as well have been
a lighted arrow over his head saying *he's the murderer. Arrest him.*

She started to crumple the letter, then stopped,
and instead folded it and tucked it back into the envelope. She stuck the envelope into the folder, just
in case Wheatly didn't stop contacting her and she
had to pursue some kind of legal action. Either way,
she would forget about what he'd said. When John
David Wheatly went to prison, Kate had made a sol-
emn promise over Luke's grave that she would hold
no malice for Wheatly and would give him no room
in her mind or heart ever again.

A promise that was hard to keep when every time
she turned around there was a chilling reminder of
Wheatly right in front of her eyes.

The Blue Ridge Barbecue was quiet for a week-
night, with only a handful of cars in the parking lot.
She'd arrived ten minutes early anyway, and as she
parked in the lot, she saw Mack Snyder's dark brown
sedan swing into a space nearby. When she got out

of the car, he did too. He spied her and a bemused smile curved across his face. "We're both early."

"I hate to be late for anything," she said. "It makes me feel like my whole day has been thrown off-kilter."

Mack's smile seemed to fill his entire face. The waves of his dark hair had been tamed, his shirt pressed and his shoes polished. He looked nice. Very nice. "What do you know? We have something in common. Guess that means we have to be friends now."

That coaxed a laugh out of her. "Friends sounds like a step in the right direction." Wasn't that what she wanted? But as she stared at this man who had also dressed up for their night, she had to wonder if either one of them would classify this as a friends-only evening.

A heartbeat passed between them. "Well," he said, clearing his throat. "Let's go get some dinner and see if we can make some headway on everything else."

The hostess seated them in a booth near the back of the restaurant, far from the noises of the kitchen and the other diners. Kate tugged her folder for the Lily Ridge case out of her tote bag and set it on the table. It was thicker this time than it had been a week ago and would grow even bigger as she kept re-searching. On his side of the table, Mack had placed a three-ring binder only slightly thicker than her folder. Lily's name and a case number were written in marker on the spine.

The binder wasn't the only thing she noticed.

Mack Snyder was impossible to miss. He'd changed from his usual polo shirt and put on a light blue dress shirt which made him look relaxed, less stern, almost…fun. He had on dark jeans instead of the khakis she'd seen him in before. And if she wasn't mistaken, he was also wearing cologne. Something dark and woodsy. Maybe she hadn't been the only one nervous about classifying this meeting as dating or not.

"So, I had the library run me a report on that book." Mack pulled a paper out of his binder. "Lily has never checked it out of the library. In fact, no one checked it out for a year before Luke did."

She scanned the paper. Her heart did a little hitch when she saw Luke's name in print. Every once in a while, the loss hit her like a surprise left hook. She realized this *A Walk in the Woods* was likely the very last book Luke read, and that made her so very sad.

"Also, I've been trying to find that witness who said she saw Lily in Panama City, but I'm coming up empty. No one by that name lives there, and my father didn't take down a phone number or any contact information. I'm afraid that's a dead end," he said.

"So there's no way for us to know if that witness really saw Lily or just someone who looked like her. I do have something to share with you. I did an interview with one of Lily's friends today," she said. "Ashley Graham. Maybe you remember her from the file?"

"I do. She said she'd seen Lily at school, but that was the last time." Mack crossed his hands over the menu. His eyes were bright with interest. "Did she have anything new to add?"

"Actually, I think she did. Did you read anything in the folder about a creepy guy who might have been stalking Lily? Or did your father mention anything about that?"

Mack frowned. "I don't remember seeing anything like that. I'm sure if there'd been a report, my father would have followed up on it."

Kate wasn't so sure. The more she looked at this case, as well as Luke's and Elaine's, the more she was beginning to doubt that James Snyder was the super detective everyone thought he'd been. He hadn't followed up with Ashley, who would have been a key witness, or the witness who supposedly saw Lily. He'd left so many loose ends, the case couldn't hold itself together. "Ashley said she told the police about him. In fact, she was emphatic that she had told your father about the creepy guy. If she did, then that testimony should be in his notes from the call. And if it isn't, then your father purposely left it out and didn't bother to schedule an official statement with Ashley later. The question is why. And when is someone going to check out what Ashley said?"

Mack bristled at the criticism of his father. She could see his posture stiffen and his mouth thin into a tight line. "Kate, it's been three years. *Creepy guy* is a vague description. It could be nothing."

"And it could be something. Lily worked at the Skyview Diner." She leaned forward and lowered her voice so the other restaurant patrons didn't overhear.

"Don't you think it's worth talking to the owner to see if he remembers anything?"

He shook his head. "There won't be any surveillance video or any evidence. Not after three years."

"But there might be a clue. If Ned, the owner, remembers some guy who seemed out of place, then maybe we can get a sketch done and that can lead us to the person who took Lily."

"Whoa, whoa." Mack put up his hands and leaned back in his seat. "You are putting the cart a mile ahead of the horse. First, memory is a funny thing, and the chances of the owner remembering one particular Skyview Diner guest out of the thousands he sees during a year, especially in the height of tourist season, is pretty much zero. Secondly, the department is not going to pay for a sketch artist for a case that is officially closed. And third, you're still presuming that Lily was kidnapped."

"And you're presuming she wasn't!" Her voice was sharp and loud, and she took a moment to compose herself again. Every single part of this investigation was an uphill battle. Why didn't Mack Snyder just see her points and help her, instead of resisting her at every turn? "You don't have anything that proves she lives in Florida. You have one phone call from someone who you can't find now. Lily looked a lot like every other sixteen-year-old girl in the world. Long brown hair, big green eyes, slender, liked jeans and concert Ts. That witness could have seen anyone in that store in Panama City."

He considered her for a long moment. "You have a point. I'll go see Ned over at the Skyview tomorrow."

A rush of gratitude flooded her. Thank God he had listened and agreed to look into it. She appreciated that Mack listened to her opinions and gave them credence, even if it sometimes took a little work to get there. Maybe now they could gain some traction on Lily's disappearance. "Can I come with you?"

He chuckled. "Of course not. This is not an episode of *Castle*, Kate. This is police work and you shouldn't be involved."

"You said yourself the case is officially closed, so what harm could it do to bring me along?" She shrugged a shoulder and gave him an innocent look. "Please?"

He picked up his menu and raised it in front of his face but not before she saw amusement flicker in his eyes. "Have you eaten here recently?"

"Is that you changing the subject?"

He peered around his menu. "We started the night as friends. Let's try to end it that way too."

Something that felt a lot like disappointment echoed inside her at the word *friends*. That was crazy because being friends was a good thing. It meant Mack would work with her on the case, surely, and they wouldn't be at odds all the time. Besides, she barely had time to breathe, never mind date. "Okay," she said. "So how do we do that?"

He chuckled. "Don't ask me. I'm no better at having a personal life than you are."

"I have a personal life."

Mack arched a brow. "You work at the coffee shop, then you record the podcast, and in your spare time, you pester me. I don't think that qualifies as a personal life."

"I do not pester you." Then she dipped her head and blushed. "Okay, maybe I do, but it's for a good cause."

Mack liked the way her cheeks flushed when she felt shy. Kate wasn't a woman who got flustered easily. He suspected she kept her emotional walls high and rarely let her guard down. There were layers to Kate McAllister, and a smart man wouldn't think about anything beyond the case, but Mack wasn't being smart right now at all.

"You look very beautiful tonight," he said, and then it was his turn to feel uncomfortable. He'd never mastered flirting and didn't even know how to have game. Like Kate, he rarely let his walls down, because that was the best way to keep from getting emotionally drawn into a case. But he couldn't stop himself from staring at the blue dress and noticing the way it brought out the color of her eyes and the rich golden hues of her hair.

The flush in her cheeks deepened. "Thank you. I...well, I borrowed this from my roommate because I'm not really a dresses kind of woman. And—" her cheeks got even redder "—I have no idea why I told you all that. I am not good at this."

"You want to know a secret? Neither am I." The waitress came by their table and both of them seemed to welcome the interruption. It shifted the tension in the space into something everyday. Mack ordered the steak, while Kate got the smoked chicken. "That was going to be my second choice."

"And steak was mine." She grinned. "Guess we have two things in common."

Two seemed like a good start. If they spent more time together—time that wasn't just focused on the Lily Ridge investigation—would they discover even more commonality?

For a long time, Mack had resigned himself to being alone. He worked more hours than he should, and when he was home, he was usually either asleep or working more. Like Kate, he didn't go out much or go on guy's nights. He'd never been that kind of guy to begin with, because he preferred a quieter life without the drinking or endless dating. But a woman like Kate, who was smart and determined, and who seemed to like the same things as he did—okay, two things weren't exactly all the same things—was the kind of woman who made him rethink his solitary bachelor life.

The waitress had left behind a bowl of fresh-baked rolls, warm and glistening with their buttered tops. Mack offered the basket to Kate, then plucked out one for himself. He slathered it in butter, then popped a chunk in his mouth. The bite of bread was soft and sweet, a perfect beginning to their meal. "Do you have family here?" he asked. Even though these were answers he could easily get from the computer at work, he wanted to get to know Kate in the regular way. Have an ordinary conversation and see where that went.

"My mom died a few years ago, but my dad still lives here. The coffee shop was my mom's, and when she got sick, I came back home to run it for her." Kate smeared more butter on her roll, and Mack realized they had a third thing in common. "Then I never left."

"Where did you move to before?"

"I went to college at Chapel Hill. I loved it there and was about to take a job at a newspaper and become a journalist. I never intended to run the coffee shop. That was always my mom's thing. But now that I'm here, I realize how much I missed Fordham and how much I like being a part of the community."

"And then you met Luke and decided to settle down?"

She shook her head. "It didn't work quite like that. I was too busy when I first took over the Corner Cup to even think about dating. It was a crazy time, trying to keep the business afloat and bring back all the customers we had lost when my mother got sick. I had known Luke but only as a friend of friends. I think I saw him a half dozen times before we connected. After that, it all seemed to move so fast. He wanted to get married right away. Even though we got engaged pretty quickly, I kept putting off setting the date. I was…"

"More cautious."

"Yeah. That's pretty much my middle name."

"Mine, too, which is why I'm also still living in

Fordham and haven't settled down yet." He chuckled. "I dated a woman for two years. Really thought I'd marry her, but I don't know…it never felt quite right. She hated that I was a cop, and I think that would have been a big issue down the road."

Their salads came, then their food, and the conversation continued to flow. They talked about growing up in Fordham, about knowing of each other, but not knowing each other because they were three years apart in school. The conversation zigged and zagged through movies and TV shows, then to restaurants and amusement parks. Every subject they touched on had some kind of common connection between them. Before Mack knew it, their plates were cleared and the waitress was asking if they wanted anything else. It seemed like only five minutes had passed, when in reality it had been two hours. "I've never had a date or a meeting, or whatever this was, go by so fast."

She glanced at the clock on her phone. "Wow. We've been here for hours. It feels like we just got here and sat down."

"That's because you're so easy to talk to."

A smile curved across her face. "So are you. This might sound weird, but I feel like I know you now."

"I feel the same way." He glanced over at the file beside her and felt a twinge of guilt. The whole purpose of coming here was to focus on finding one lost teenage girl. That should be where he put his concentration, not the smile on Kate's face. "We totally got off the subject of Lily. Why don't we order coffee and dessert and talk about the case some more?"

"I'd love that. Not just because I want to find Lily, but selfishly, I…well—" the flush filled her cheeks again "—I don't want to go home yet."

Those words warmed him. It had been a long time since he'd so thoroughly enjoyed talking to a woman, a beautiful woman at that. "Me neither." He signaled to the waitress, placed their order then pulled out his binder. He couldn't think of another place he'd rather be than talking shop with Kate. How quickly they had gone from enemies to friends to something he couldn't define. "Okay, let's compare notes."

As she opened her folder, a white envelope spilled out. He saw the words *Piedmont Correctional Institute* and his radar perked. A chill ran up his spine. He knew the answer before he even asked the question, and he had to work to keep the frustration and worry out of his voice. "What is that?"

"It's nothing. It's a letter." She started to shove it back into the folder, but Mack touched her hand and stopped her.

"Did Wheatly write to you?" he asked. *Please say no. Don't let that murderer come anywhere near you.*

She waved it off as if the whole thing didn't matter, but he could hear the nervous tremble in her voice. "It's no big deal. He does it every once in a while, and my address is on the podcast site, so fans can write to me. He thinks he can convince me he's innocent, but I know better."

"First, take your address off the website immediately. You're just inviting trouble that you don't need." Mack wanted to run out of this restaurant and show up in front of Wheatly's cell, to tell him exactly why he should never contact Kate again. Instead, Mack reigned in his temper and shifted into detective mode. If Wheatly was contacting her, maybe there was some link to another crime or something Mack should know. "Can I read it?"

She hesitated, assessing him, maybe wondering how he would react. "Okay. But I don't need you to swoop in and rescue me. I have this under control."

A convicted murderer was sending her letters. Mack wouldn't call that having it under control. But he kept that to himself and unfolded the single sheet of paper. Ice ran through his veins as he read the short, pointed, menacing letter. "Somebody's going to die? This almost sounds like a threat."

"It's not. It's nothing." She plucked the letter out of his hands and folded it up again. "I shouldn't have shown you."

"Kate, you have to take this seriously. You can't take these kinds of risks. One of these days, you are going to get hurt. Wheatly is dangerous."

"He's behind bars. He can't reach me." But he could see her tremble a bit as she put the letter away.

"No, but he can pay someone on the outside who can." Mack leaned across the table. "You didn't write back, did you?"

"Of course not. I don't answer his calls or his letters." Her mouth formed a little O. "I mean—"

"He calls you too?" Mack shook his head. "And

how many letters are we talking about? This has to stop. I'm going to talk to the warden at Piedmont tomorrow."

"I don't need you jumping in to fight my battles, Detective. All I want to do is find Lily." Her posture stiffened and her tone, so warm and inviting before, went cold and distant.

Every instinct inside him screamed to protect her. Against his better judgment, he nodded. Kate was an adult, and, like any adult, didn't want him telling her what to do or how to run her life. "Okay. But until then, will you tell me if Wheatly contacts you or threatens you in any way?"

"He hasn't threatened me, exactly. Don't blow this up into something it isn't. He's just protesting his innocence like lots of guilty people do. I saw Luke's car in his yard. I know he isn't innocent at all. And I'm not going to give him the satisfaction of a response."

"Good. I'm glad to hear it." Although he wasn't quite certain that Kate would stick to her promise. This was, after all, the same woman who had parked in Wheatly's driveway and tried to confront him about Winslow's car. Thank God the police had showed up in time to stop her from such foolishness. Kate was passionate about what she did, but that passion could also be foolhardy. "Now tell me more about Ashley."

"I thought you didn't believe me about her."

"I never said that. Maybe she did tell the police about this creepy guy, and maybe she didn't. Either way, I am not the kind of cop who leaves a stone unturned." Not to mention, the more he heard from Kate, the more he wondered if his father had just coasted on this investigation. He'd retired thirteen months after the Winslow and Ridge cases. Maybe Dad was tired and didn't give this case his all, or maybe he'd grown jaded by the job and skated by on the last few cases. Hard to believe, given James Snyder's reputation, but either way, Mack needed to dig deeper, if only for his own peace of mind. His father, after all, had told him more than once that the only way to be a good cop was to follow every bit of evidence.

If that was James's personal motto, then why would he mess up on this case? It simply didn't make sense.

Either way, whether Kate wanted him to or not, Mack was going to keep an eye on her and make sure Wheatly didn't send her so much as a carrier pigeon.

Chapter Nine

The hand on Kate's arm stopped her in the middle of turning the key to lock the shop. In an instant, her breath stopped, and the urge to scream raced up her throat. She spun around, pulse racing, fear pulsing inside her, then just as quickly, she calmed. "Mrs. Reynolds. You scared me."

"I'm so sorry. I just wanted to get your attention." Elaine's mother seemed flustered and embarrassed to have startled Kate.

Downtown Fordham was quiet, save for the occasional car. Kate had just closed the coffee shop and had opted to walk home, given the warm, sunny day made brighter and sweeter by a morning rain. She'd been lost in her thoughts, musing about the dinner with Mack, and not really paying attention as she left work. It was so unlike her to have her head in the clouds, as her grandmother would have called it. Which was all the more reason to refocus on her work, and not on the detective.

"I wanted to say hello," Helen Reynolds said, "and thank you again for bringing attention to my daughter's case."

Attention that had gone sideways pretty quickly. All those listeners, descending on Fordham, thinking they were going to crowdsource the answer to what happened to Elaine last season. The accident at the pharmacy, the bad publicity and then the police department issuing her a warning all happened in the space of a couple days. One week later, Elaine's body had been found by a creek, with a single bullet wound to the temple, and the whole thing was ruled a suicide. Such a tragic end to a troubled woman who was only in her early thirties.

Kate covered Helen's hand with her own. Grief clouded the older woman's eyes, and sadness weighed down her shoulders. Losing a child, at any age, had to be the most devastating thing in the world. "I only wish we didn't have to do it all."

"Well, there are a lot of people who will remember Elaine now because of what you did and how nicely you spoke about her on your show." Helen brightened by a degree. "And I have answers. They're not the answers I wanted, but they are something."

There'd been no note left behind by Elaine, no way to tie up the loose ends and answer the rest of Helen's haunting questions. Elaine had been suicidal in the past and battled depression and a drug addiction. She'd get her life together, then something would happen—a breakup, a job loss, a sudden move—and she'd fall off the wagon again. Twice, she had tried overdosing on pills, and twice her mother had saved her. This last time, maybe Elaine had driven off to a remote spot where she wouldn't be found or stopped. Maybe that explained the gun instead of pills too. Either way, it was a terrible loss.

When she first started covering the Reynolds case, Kate had been so sure Elaine had been murdered, and so committed to finding justice. So many clues had pointed to foul play, but the autopsy held the only answer—a gunshot wound to her temple. Breaking the news to her viewers had been tough, but having the conversation with Helen had been even worse. How brave Helen had been to come on the podcast and talk about her daughter, urging people to get help if they were struggling with suicidal thoughts. Kate could only pray those shows had made a difference for at least one person, and they reached out for help instead of taking their own lives. "How are you doing?"

"One day at a time. Sometimes one hour at a time." She shrugged, and her eyes filled with tears. "It never gets easier to lose a child."

Kate drew Elaine's mother into a hug. Other people strolled past them, on their way to families and dinners and memories. All Elaine's mother had was this moment. "I'm so sorry."

Helen drew back and swiped at her eyes. "It's fine. Anyway, I just wanted to say hello."

"It's always nice to see you, and I greatly appreciate your kind words." Kate turned back to finish locking the door. As she went to drop her keys into her pocket, a snippet of conversation from a year ago came back. "Helen, didn't Elaine work at the Skyview Diner?"

"She was the head server for ten years." A wistful look came over Helen's features. "That place was like a second family to her."

The Skyview was a couple miles away from Fordham, a convenient pull-off from the Blue Ridge Parkway. It was the typical small-town diner: locally owned, dependable menu and a popular stop for locals and out-of-towners, especially on weekend mornings. "Do you think she knew Lily Ridge?"

Helen thought for a moment. "That's the girl who ran away a few years ago, right?"

"Well, we think she didn't run away." She'd used the word *we*, unconsciously including Mack in the abduction theory. When had she started thinking of him as part of her investigation? "But yes, that's the girl."

"I remember Elaine mentioning her when she disappeared. I don't think she knew her well because Elaine mostly worked mornings and a girl that young would have worked afternoons, but I do know my daughter was worried about the girl. Actually, come to think of it, I think Elaine worked Saturdays with Lily. I remember her saying that the girl was a great waitress, but she needed to have a better attitude. Teenagers, you know?"

Kate tugged a notebook out of her tote bag and made a couple notes, reminding herself to check with the diner's owner about Lily's schedule. "Did Elaine ever mention a creepy guy coming on to Lily at the Skyview?"

"Not that I can think of. But there was always someone who made Elaine feel uncomfortable. With that place being right off the highway, you get a lot of tourists and truck drivers, and every once in a while there would be someone who would make her nervous." A wistful smile flickered on Helen's face. "But my Elaine was always very careful."

"Well, if you think of anything she might have said back then, let me know. One of Lily's friends mentioned something about a creepy guy. It might be nothing," she said, thinking of Mack's words, "but I still want to check into it."

"Of course. Anything I can do to help you." Helen put a hand on Kate's arm, stopping her before she put the notebook away. "When you said that about the creepy guy, you reminded me of something else. Something the police department told me was nothing."

Kate's spine tingled. Maybe this detail was one that could lead her to Lily. To answers. She unfolded the cover of the notebook and clicked her pen. "What was it?"

"When that coroner, what was his name?"

"Josephs." Incompetent was too generous of a word to describe the former coroner. He'd been assigned to Luke's autopsy, too, and from the notes Kate had seen, he'd done the bare minimum of an exam.

"When he did Elaine's autopsy, he hardly examined her," Helen said, as if she was an echo of Kate's thoughts.

Two bad autopsies? How many others had Josephs skated by on? The police department was well rid of him. The only question was why they hadn't seen his ineptitude earlier. "That's part of why he was fired. He took the easiest way out possible every single time."

"Which is what he did with my Elaine, but I didn't know that until just this week. I was at a wake for a friend of mine that was held at the same funeral home I used for Elaine's service. The funeral director, Mort, pulled me aside and asked to talk to me." Helen shifted to the left to let a woman with a stroller pass by. "He was the one who personally took care of my little girl, because we know each other. Not well, but well enough. Two years ago, Mort told me he couldn't bring himself to share what he saw when he prepared her for the viewing. I told him it was okay to tell me what he needed to."

"You're so brave," Kate said. "I know this must have been a hard conversation to have, even after two years."

"It always is. But talking about Elaine keeps her here." Helen tapped the space over her heart. "Even if I'm talking about the bad parts."

Exactly what Kate had felt when she was on that microphone week after week, talking about Luke, and the exact reason why she had chosen to talk about what happened to Lily Ridge. If the names of the missing and dead were still spoken, were they really gone? "What did Mort tell you?"

Helen paused a beat, then let out a long breath. For all her courage, sharing the details of her daughter's autopsy was clearly painful. "Mort said Josephs didn't cut her open, and at first when he said that, I was glad because I didn't want anyone to hurt my little girl, you know? Even though I knew she was gone, it just…" Helen shrugged a little. "Anyway, then Mort told me how unusual it was for any coroner to skip that step. Then he said something I didn't quite understand. The gunshot wound to Elaine's head seemed…off somehow."

"Off? What did he mean by that?" Kate made a note, adding a question mark after *off*.

"Well, the wound was on the left side of her head, which made sense because she was left-handed, but Mort thought it was angled wrong. Like Elaine would have had to reach up to do it." Helen tapped the top of her temple. "Most people who…well, do what Elaine did, shoot dead on, not down. I mean, it's probably nothing…"

"Maybe she slipped and fell and that affected the shot? She was found on the bottom of that hill by the creek, and she could have tripped while she was… you know. The cops think that's why they couldn't find the gun, because it tumbled into the water."

"Maybe. And maybe I'm just making a mountain out of a molehill because life is hard without my daughter here." Helen gave Kate a small smile. "Have a wonderful night, Kate, and keep up the good fight."

"I'm trying." Kate watched Helen turn and head back to her car. Kate lingered on the sidewalk, her mind whirring. There was a detail buried in what Helen had told her, something that she was missing. Whatever the connection was, it lingered just out of reach. Kate studied her notes, but they offered no more insight than she already had. Maybe there was no connection to find, or maybe she just needed to go home, get some sleep and, as Helen said, start the good fight again bright and early tomorrow.

The last thing Mack needed was a strawberry scone. He'd been so busy these last two weeks that he'd only managed to fit in one run, which meant his stress level and his waistline were both going to be increasing. And that meant his decision to go into the Corner Cup early the next morning was completely irrational.

Then Kate swiveled her attention toward the door, their eyes met and he knew exactly why he was here. She'd lingered at the edge of his every thought ever since that dinner. He could barely remember what he'd eaten, but he remembered every second of their conversation.

"Good morning." A smile filled her face. She had her hair back in a ponytail again today, giving her a youngish air when paired with her bright pink T-shirt and jeans. "I saved a scone for you."

The thoughtfulness of her action touched him. Everything he learned about Kate made him like her more and more and had him wondering if maybe she liked him too. "You must have read my mind. I've been dreaming about those scones since I woke up. Although my waist doesn't need any more of them." He patted his belly.

"One scone never hurt anyone." She turned to put it in the convection oven and toast the top slightly. While the scone was warming, Kate poured him a cup of coffee. Her assistant Jeremy, a college kid with a mop of dark hair and a ready smile for everyone, was busy at the other end of the counter filling orders.

Mack slipped onto one of the bar stools. "Thanks for the coffee. Do you have a minute? I wanted to talk to you about what Ashley said."

"Sure. Just give me five minutes to help Jeremy finish up these orders and then I can take a break."

He watched her help the customers with a friendly but efficient air. She moved quickly, but kept up a continual patter of conversation. She knew the names of her customers' kids and asked about one lady's cat, another man's dog. Clearly people came to the Corner Cup for more than just amazing scones and great coffee.

When the orders were filled, Kate tugged off the apron around her waist, poured herself a cup of coffee then gestured for Mack to follow her. They skirted the sofas and tables that peppered the shop, then walked out the back door and onto a small patio that held a trio of tables and one long wooden bench. The air was a bit brisk, but the sun was bright, and it warmed their backs when they sat down.

"I talked to the owner of the Skyview Diner yesterday," he said. "And he doesn't remember anyone specifically making Lily uncomfortable. If that happened, she never said anything to him."

"Maybe she was embarrassed or thought she could handle it alone."

"Very possible. Lots of people do that, instead of trusting their instincts." Mack set his coffee on the ledge of the bench. "I know you were hoping that this would be a lead, but there's nothing to pursue."

"Maybe." Kate fiddled with her mug. "But we need to look into everything, right?"

Mack nodded. "I also talked to my sister again. She knew Lily from the study group she ran over at Fordham High. She said she doesn't remember Lily mentioning anything about anyone following her, but she did say that Lily seemed really troubled after she came home from the youth group retreat."

"That would have been just a couple weeks before she disappeared. Ashley said something had upset Lily while she was on the retreat but she didn't want to talk to anyone but Luke about it." Which meant whatever had been bothering Lily had died with Luke. How Kate wished she'd had a longer conversation with him when he came home, asked more questions, shown more interest. She'd been too busy with work, and too sure there would be another time for a conversation with Luke.

Kate sat down, drew her knees up to her chest and clutched her coffee with both hands. "I ran into Elaine Reynolds's mother yesterday afternoon, and she said something that got me thinking. I know, I know, the cases aren't related. Except for the fact that Elaine and Lily worked together."

"They did?"

She nodded. "Lily disappeared shortly after she started working at the Skyview Diner. Helen said that Elaine never mentioned anyone creepy specifically, but that there were a lot of out-of-towners and strangers who would stop in, and several made her uncomfortable."

"That's still not enough to go on." Mack popped a bite of scone into his mouth and made a *mmm* sound. Mack loved her silly scones, and that pleased Kate on a hundred different levels.

Kate jerked her mind back to the subject at hand. "Well, this is probably nothing, but Helen said something else that was interesting. Elaine's autopsy, as we both know from the case file, was barely an exam. Doc Josephs just decided she was a suicide and left it at that. He never went any further."

"Which is exactly why he no longer works for the department. You know, it's a shame. Josephs was, for all intents and purposes, a decent coroner right up until the last couple years. Then he seemed to slip…a lot. More with each case." Mack ate another bite, then washed it down with some coffee. "These scones really are spectacular."

"Thanks." Kate gave him a smile. "Well, uh, Helen said the funeral director told her the other day that the wound was all wrong. He didn't tell Helen what he noticed at the time of the funeral because she was burying her daughter and that was all she could handle, but now that a couple years have passed, he thought he should mention that he found it odd that the entrance wound was high up on her head, like she was shooting herself from above, instead of dead-on."

Mack seemed to mull that over in his mind for a little bit. "That's an awkward way to shoot yourself, but things like that do happen. It doesn't mean anything, Kate, and it doesn't have anything to do with Lily."

"I know. But..." She hesitated. There were all these pieces whirling around in her mind, but she couldn't seem to put them together. Pieces of Luke's story, of Elaine's, of Lily's. All these awkward jigsaw puzzle pieces that didn't want to fit. And in the midst of them was one person.

"But what?"

She cupped her mug with both hands, warming her fingers against the chill in the air. "Don't you find it odd that three of your father's cases have had minimal investigations? You and I can disagree about Luke's case, but Elaine's autopsy should have been followed up on. You said yourself that Josephs only got bad at his job in the last couple years. Wouldn't your dad have noticed that and said something? Ordered a second autopsy at least? At the very least, there should have been some questions asked. Lily's case file is incomplete, and that's a generous word for how much is missing."

The urge to leap to his father's defense was strong,

but even Mack couldn't deny that Kate had a point. Maybe his father had gotten sloppy as he got closer to retirement, or maybe he dropped the ball a couple of times. Maybe that was why Dad was so defensive when Mack asked him about the cases.

For decades, his father's investigative abilities had been praised by the Fordham Police Department. But even heroes made mistakes, and even the best struggled to perform well every single time. His father's reputation was an impossible standard for Mack to rise to, which made the thought of questioning anything James did almost seem like a betrayal. What did Mack know? He'd been a detective for a couple years, not even long enough to get his feet wet.

But three cases? That was so out of character for his father. Maybe he needed to pay another visit to Dad. Mack had worked parts of the Elaine Reynolds case with his father and hadn't seen a note about the entry wound angle. Then again, Mack had been assigned to cataloging the items from the scene and canvassing the people who lived near where Elaine was found. With both Luke's and Elaine's cases, Dad had given Mack menial chores to do. He'd invited his son along under the guise of helping him learn how to investigate, but in reality, Mack had been a step above a gopher. Was that because his father didn't want anyone to see that he was losing his touch?

"You said she seemed to have shot herself on the top of her head?" he asked.

"Yeah, why?"

A thought remained just out of reach in Mack's

mind. A thread he was missing or another that was unraveling. Whatever it was, he couldn't quite grasp it. "Nothing. Just something about what you said is nagging me."

"The same thing happened to me when Helen told me about the autopsy. I felt like there was something I should remember. But I don't know what it is. Maybe it's just that Doc Josephs stopped caring what kind of job he did."

"That would be a fact," Mack said. "Chief Richmond has been going over many of Doc's old cases. Only a handful have been treated as badly as Elaine's and Luke's, but even a handful is too many."

"That kind of incompetence could cost the police department an arrest," Kate said. "And could put the wrong man in jail."

He wondered if Wheatly's letters had affected her more than she'd let on. After all, Kate was the main reason Wheatly had been arrested in the first place. If she hadn't been in his driveway, Wheatly might have taken off and never been seen again. "Speaking of people in jail, I'm also going to go talk to John David Wheatly today." He held up his hand when she started to protest. "I'm not doing it to try to micromanage you, Kate. It's my job to prevent crime as much as it is to solve crimes. If Wheatly is threatening another murder, I need to get to the bottom of it."

"I think I should come along. And before you immediately say no, think about it. You're a cop, and part of why he's in that prison. He's not going to be inclined to open up to you. For whatever reason, he wants to talk to me and has been trying to do so for months. I'll be right there beside you, and he'll be separated from us by a glass wall. Nothing will happen, Mack."

She looked so earnest and vulnerable in that moment. He wanted to shield Kate from anything that could harm her, but he also knew when to face reality. He was a cop, and not only could that be intimidating to Wheatly, it might stop the whole interview before it even happened.

"I hate to admit that you have a point. I don't know why Wheatly has reached out to you, but if he's willing to open up, maybe we can prevent someone else from getting hurt." He finished the last bite of scone. "I have to get back to work. Does one o'clock work for going over to Piedmont? I'll pick you up and we can ride together."

"Perfect. Jeremy wanted extra hours this week, so I know I can get him to cover."

"And Kate, one more thing." He met her gaze and held it. "You need to follow my lead. Wheatly is a dangerous man with a vicious temper. Even with a glass wall between us, I don't trust him. My biggest priority is to protect you."

"As much as I'm tempted to say I can take care of myself, I appreciate that, Mack. It's nice to know you have my back." She smiled. "You're a good man."

The compliment took him by surprise. His throat thickened and, for a second, he was at a loss for words. His parents had never been particularly demonstrative or complimentary, and hearing her say such a simple thing hit him with a wave of emotion. He cleared his throat and gave her a nod. "Be ready at one."

Then he turned on his heel and left, keeping all those warm thoughts to himself, because it was easier and safer to retreat to his comfortable solitary emotional island.

Chapter Ten

The three-hour drive to Piedmont passed in a blur. Kate had run home to change out of her work shirt and into black slacks and a light V-neck sweater, something comfortable and nondescript. Mack arrived ten minutes early, but she was already waiting on the curb outside the shop. As they sped down I-40, the conversation between them flowed as easily as it had at dinner.

They'd had similar childhoods with distant, judgmental fathers, another commonality that seemed to explain why they got along so well. Kate had never met anyone who understood her complicated relationship with her father quite as well as Mack did. They'd both loved English and hated Algebra, but where he'd excelled in Biology and Chemistry, she'd dreaded science classes.

He asked her about the coffee shop, with inquisitive questions about what she loved and what challenged her most in her business. Maybe it was the detective in him, but he seemed to remember everything she'd ever said and get right to the heart of what she was saying with his comments.

"You certainly have a knack for understanding people and getting them to open up." She grinned. "I am not a person who shares my thoughts or emotions easily, and yet I've told you my whole life story on this car ride."

"And I appreciate you trusting me with all of that. I guess it's an occupational hazard. I'm curious about what makes people tick. And even more curious when it comes to people I like."

There was silence for a moment, as she tried to tame the rush of heat in her cheeks and the little joyful jig in her heart at the words *people I like*. "So, uh, tell me about you. Why did you go into police work?"

"A big part of it was wanting to be like my dad. He seemed to have such an exciting job, but also one that made him work long hours. I started asking questions about his cases when I was young, and those conversations were a way for us to sort of bond. He's always been closer to my sister, and much harder on me, maybe because I'm the boy and the oldest. He's a hard man to please, and I think a part of me wanted to make him proud by following in his footsteps."

"And is he? Proud of you?"

"Like I said, he's difficult to please. He makes it clear that he thinks I could be better at my job. Better at everything, frankly."

Sympathy ran through Kate. She knew how tough it was to have an unsupportive parent. Maybe James

Snyder was just too sold on himself as the perfect detective to see the smart, caring son he had. "I think he's wrong. You've been openminded and sympathetic and inquisitive. Those are the best traits in a detective, if you ask me."

He chuckled. "You have complimented me so much today, my head is barely going to fit through the door at Piedmont."

She studied his profile, the squareness of his jaw, the close-cropped hair and the dark eyes she'd grown to really like. "I get the feeling you aren't complimented nearly often enough."

Mack swallowed hard and shifted all of his focus to the road, as if it was too hard to look at her. "We're, uh, close to the prison now. Just remember, follow my lead and let me be in charge of this conversation with Wheatly."

The deft change of subject didn't fool her. Mack avoided emotions like some people avoided snakes. No doubt part of that was due to his job and the necessity of separating emotion from fact. Occupational hazard, to be sure, but also maybe a way to guard his heart after too many disappointments and hurts. That was another thing Kate could relate to and sympathize with because she was much the same. Either way, it was a topic for another day, but even as they parked and walked up to the imposing prison, she found her heart softening more and more toward Mack.

There was a whole process to visiting a prisoner, Kate soon discovered. Getting inside the prison to the visitor's room involved stopping for Mack to hand his gun over to the guards at the front gate, then the two of them going through a metal detector, a pat-down search and a thirty-minute wait for the guards to bring Wheatly to a stool on the other side of the glass partition.

A chill ran down Kate's spine when she saw him. Wheatly's hair was longer, his beard now full instead of the stubble he'd had at trial, but he had the same icy blue eyes and aggressive stare that she remembered. She was sitting on a second stool beside Mack, and without thinking, she reached over and grabbed his hand. He gave her fingers a reassuring squeeze.

Wheatly yanked up the phone while Mack picked up the other end, and Kate leaned in to hear the conversation. "You didn't need to bring along a police dog with you."

Mack bristled at the words. "I'm Detective Mack Snyder, and I'm here to talk to you about—"

"Ah, the chip off the old block huh?" Wheatly grinned. "Hope you're smarter than your old man, because he's the idiot who put me in this place." Then his attention swiveled toward Kate. "And I see you must have gotten my letters. About time you responded."

"I did. I, uh, wanted to talk to you about it." She glanced at Mack. On the way over here, they had rehearsed the conversation, hoping to steer it in a direction that gave Mack information he could act upon. She had to act like she believed Wheatly could be innocent, instead of showing him how much she despised him for killing Luke. She prayed her true emotions didn't show on her face or in her voice. "Why do you say you didn't commit the murder?"

"Because I didn't. You just rushed to judge me. This whole town did. I was framed, and I can prove it, but I'm not handing over that evidence without some assurances. That car was dumped in my yard, just one more junker in the pile. I didn't even know it was there until the cops busted down my door."

She bristled but kept her voice calm and controlled. There was no way Wheatly was framed. Who would want to do that? Wheatly was a cranky loner who was known for shooting his gun when the mood struck him, like when someone accidentally parked too close to his street. Whatever had made Luke stop on the side of the road that day had undoubtedly been the trigger behind Wheatly's impulsive murder. For now, Kate pretended none of that was in her mind. "Then who do you think did it if you didn't?"

A crafty smile curved along Wheatly's face. "I bet you two would love to know that answer, wouldn't you? I'll tell you what. Mr. Cop, you go put in a word with the DA and tell him I want a new trial. My lawyer's got an appeal just waiting to be heard, and if you could give the judge a nudge, I will gladly give you some information."

"That's not gonna—"

"We'll see what we can do," Kate interrupted, which made Mack shoot her a look of frustration. Yes, she'd said she would follow his lead, but his instant refusal of Wheatly's offer would get them nowhere. "Tell us something, and then we have some leverage with the judge to prove that you want to help catch the real killer."

Wheatly considered the two of them for a long time. In the background, the prison was controlled chaos. Shouts and banging, the heavy thud of doors sliding shut, the buzz of another one opening. Prisoners shuffled in and out of the visiting area, while family members waited on the hard metal stools for a few minutes of conversation. "I ain't gonna give you what I got, because it's my ticket out of here. I will tell you that when you find that girl, you'll know it wasn't me what killed the Winslow guy, or anyone else."

Kate lunged toward the window. "What girl? Lily Ridge? What does any of that have to do with Luke?"

Wheatly just smiled, then got up off the stool and turned toward the guard. He strolled out of the visitor area and disappeared behind a heavy steel door, taking whatever other answers he had with him.

Mack shook his head and let out a gust of frustration. "I think he's trying to manipulate you, Kate. He doesn't know anything about Lily. He was already in custody before she disappeared, and we know that except for the book, there is nothing tying Luke's murder to Lily's disappearance."

Kate turned to Mack. "But what if he does know something, Mack? What if Wheatly is the one who can bring her home?"

Mack glanced at the thick dark gray door that divided the cells from the visiting area. "Then we're going to have to find another way to get the information because the last thing I'm doing is getting that murderer released from prison."

He was wasting his time.

That's what Mack told himself as he carried two more boxes back from the evidence locker and placed them on top of the one containing everything to do with Lily Ridge. He wrestled the lid off the banker box marked Elaine Reynolds, pulled out the binder of testimony and reports then sat back in his chair to read.

Just as he did, his mother called him. "What's up, Ma?"

"I haven't heard from you in a couple days. I was worried about you."

"I've been working on a case." He rose to flip through the box of evidence, and noticed this box, too, was sparse. Maybe because the case had been ruled a suicide? But that had been after several weeks of searching for Elaine. Surely there would be more evidence to show how exhaustive the search had been. "Let me ask you something."

"Anything, dear. Oh, I forgot, I'm supposed to be leaving for the garden club in a minute. Thank goodness I'm riding with Alice McKnight and she's always late. But that means we'll probably miss the sprout exchange. That's when we trade new seedlings—"

"This will only take a minute." He paused before he asked the question, because he knew that once he dipped down this path, he'd be opening a door he might not want to open. "Do you think Dad was always thorough in his work? Like, was he really the cop everyone says he was?"

There was a long silence. "You know I don't like speaking ill of your father. I vowed after the divorce that I would not interfere in your relationship with him."

"I'm an adult now, Ma. Any relationship he and I have is on us, not you."

"I don't know what happened with your father's job after we got divorced. But there were some instances that I wondered about for a long time." She let out a deep breath. "When your father first got on the force, they got a domestic call. A guy he knew was beating up his wife. The wife wanted to press charges. I think she even had a broken nose from their altercation."

"Okay, sounds like a normal night."

"It was. And with most of the people that your father investigated for such things, he was hard on them. If the woman wouldn't press charges, your dad would talk to the DA, see if there was another way to put this guy behind bars. He didn't want to see anyone hurt and he was almost a crusader for that. Except this time."

"What was different?"

"You know your dad played football in high school, right? That team was close, like best-friends close. It was part of the way the coach built them into a team that went to the state semifinals. Back then, he lived, ate and slept football and that team. He's still good friends with a lot of those men. And this guy, the one who broke his wife's nose, was a running back for the team. Your dad knew him well."

"He gave a pass to a friend of his. While I think it's wrong, especially when it comes to domestic violence, sadly, it's not uncommon, Ma."

"This was more than that. I ran into the wife a couple weeks later, and she had a black eye. Everyone in town knew what her husband had done. It's the curse of living in a small town. I pulled her aside and asked her why he didn't go to jail the first night. She said, and I'll never forget this, 'that cop told me that pressing charges would be a very bad idea. I was more scared of him than I was of my husband, so I dropped it.'" The sound of a double beep from a car horn sounded in the background. "That's Alice, so I have to go. I don't know if that story answers your question or not. It's always bothered me that your father puts loyalty ahead of the law."

"Thanks, Ma. I don't really know what answer I was looking for, but I appreciate you talking to me."

"Just promise me you'll be careful, Mack. I worry about you all the time." She told him she loved him, gave him a hard time about not visiting more often then hung up.

Mack reopened the Reynolds file, searching through the few documents inside the folder. There wasn't much to go on, at least from an investigative standpoint. The autopsy was, as Helen had said, barely completed, with only a cursory report. The anatomical drawing had made a note of the left-entry high-on-the-temple gunshot wound, but Josephs hadn't written any conclusions about the odd entry wound. He hadn't checked for gunshot residue on her hands, and the weapon was never found. Josephs had merely checked the box marked *suicide* and seemed to call the report done.

The chief found him in the same place an hour later. He paused and scanned the names on the evidence boxes. "I know I told you to follow your hunches, but this looks like you're throwing spaghetti at the wall. You have a murder, a suicide and a runaway. None of those are related. We already arrested the murderer, the family buried the suicide and the runaway is…doing whatever runaway girls do instead of calling their families."

Mack rubbed at his chin. His five-o'clock shadow was giving way to a scruffy beard, a clear sign he'd been working too many hours. "Did you read Doc's report on Elaine?"

"The one that he barely did?" The chief nodded. "It was a poor excuse for an autopsy. I would have ordered an independent one, but your father was positive it was a suicide."

Which meant the higher-ups had probably not done their own review of the case. They'd trusted the veteran detective's work, probably grateful for the easy answer, and then moved on to the next case.

"You know, Josephs screwed up a few times before he was fired, but I went through his last five years of cases, and only a few were sloppy like this," Chief Richmond said. "I think he got into some financial trouble or something. Maybe that affected his work. He was a great coroner for fifteen years before he started slipping up."

Mack opened the binder, flipped to the photo of Elaine on the morgue's table and turned it around to face his boss. "Do you notice anything wrong with this picture?"

He studied it for a moment. "That entry wound is a bit high." The chief picked up the image and looked more closely. "She must have had her hand cocked at an odd angle."

"Maybe." Mack pulled out a sheet of paper that contained the notes his father had written after the interview with the family. "When my fath—uh, Detective Snyder—asked the family about what might have made Elaine commit suicide, they had mentioned many things that had gone wrong in her life recently. A long-term relationship had ended, she'd had a small relapse with drugs, stuff like that. She attempted suicide twice before, but with pills, and she'd always written a note. To switch to a remote location and a gun? And not leave a note? Seems inconsistent to me."

"People do crazy things, Snyder." Chief Richmond narrowed his gaze and took a closer look at the photo. "But you're right. It is inconsistent with her earlier pattern."

"But this…" Mack reached into another box and pulled out a second binder. "This one makes even less sense." He turned to the autopsy for Luke Winslow. Josephs had done a more thorough job on Luke, maybe because the case was clearly a murder. The prosecutor had put together a timeline that said Wheatly must have flagged down Luke while he was driving along Soco Gap, then tackled him, as evidenced by the scuffling of footsteps in the sandy dirt, the gravel scrapes on Luke's hands and a bruise on Luke's shoulder. Wheatly had shot Luke in the head, then stolen Luke's cell phone and wallet. Luke Winslow was not a rich man, which meant he'd been killed for the few dollars he'd had in his pocket. But when put side by side with the anatomical drawing for Elaine Reynolds, Mack saw an eerie coincidence.

He pointed to the coroner's sketch of the wound, then to the picture of the hole in Luke's skull. "Winslow was shot in almost exactly the same place, by the same caliber weapon. We never found a gun at the scene or in Wheatly's house."

"Because he ditched it after he shot Winslow." The chief shrugged. "Give Wheatly credit for one smart move, but he's no Boy Scout. You've seen his rap sheet. I'm convinced he's good for this murder, and a jury of his peers agreed. Don't tell me you're thinking that guy is innocent?"

"No, definitely not." As the boss had said, Wheatly had the criminal background to prove he wasn't above violence to get what he wanted. Mainly it had been threats with the gun, and beating a few shopkeepers up, but not murder. Every criminal, however, was not a murderer until they were, and maybe Winslow had been Wheatly's first kill. Still, the odd similarity to Elaine Reynolds bothered him.

Wheatly had been locked up when she died, which meant he had nothing to do with Elaine's death. "But the deaths are pretty similar. Look closer at the photos and tell me you see it too."

"I'll admit, those wounds do look a lot alike." He handed the book back to Mack. "But your dad investigated these, and he was one heck of a detective. I can understand him having a bad day, but there's no way he had two or three bad cases in a row."

Mack nodded. "Maybe so. But it seems like I should look into this. I have questions that I need answered."

"I think the first question you should ask yourself is why your father, who was one of the most conscientious and meticulous men I've ever met, would get something this big so horribly wrong? Are you sure it's not some backward motivation to prove the old man wrong?"

The chief's words echoed with the doubt in Mack's mind. Were his motives pure? Was he doing this to get to the truth, or to make himself shine above his perfect father? Could there be an ulterior motive driving Mack to see things that weren't there? "I… I just think there's something here. I can't put my finger on it."

"You've got open investigations that need your attention, Snyder. Following a hunch or two is one thing, but putting the robberies and break-ins aside to redo work that has already been done is another." The chief waved at the pile on the table. "Put those boxes back and get to work on the crimes we need to solve. That's an order."

"Yes, sir." After the chief left, Mack picked up all the boxes and headed down the hall toward the evidence room to re-shelve everything and go back to doing his job. That had been, after all, a direct order, and a detective who wanted to make his mark within the police department didn't do so by disobeying.

I built my reputation on following the leads, Mack, and on doing good police work. Don't go undoing all that with a wild goose chase.

His father's words danced in and out around his doubts. He thought of what his mother had said, about how his father had done the wrong thing at least once. Was there a possibility that James Snyder wasn't as perfect as everyone thought? And what good would exposing his father's mistakes do?

He should let it go. Put the evidence away and follow orders. This investigation was either going to waste a colossal amount of time or lead to an outcome no one would like.

Mack glanced down the hall, hesitated only a second longer, then took a left toward the copier. Two minutes later, he stowed the evidence boxes back on their shelves and returned to his desk and the endless mountain of paperwork that was the true job of any cop.

The stark black letters, bolded and in all caps, screamed at her from the flat laptop screen. *I SAW YOU TALKING TO HIM. YOU WILL PAY THE*

PRICE WHEN YOU LEAST EXPECT IT. JUST LIKE THAT STUPID GIRL DID AND THE OTHERS BEFORE HER. —Wary Watcher.

Kate's hand shook as she scrolled her mouse to the corner of the screen and hovered over the *X* that would close the window. No. She refused to be intimidated by this anonymous poster. He had hidden behind his anonymity to make threats that were undoubtedly empty. In the online forum for crime podcasters she belonged to, many of them talked about crazy fans who spouted theories and threats, just to generate some conversation on the show, a backward way of getting their fifteen minutes of fame. She wouldn't give Wary Watcher the satisfaction of hearing his insanity on the air, but she also wasn't going to let him think he was getting to her.

I know who you are, she typed. *You don't scare me.* There. Maybe he'd think she had some kind of tracking software on the website and he'd stop trolling her.

She hit Print, and as the inkjet whirred through the letters, she studied the message again. *I saw you talking to him.* Him who? Mack? Wheatly? Except for her customers, there'd been no other males that Kate had conversations with in the past few days. And why would Wary Watcher care? What did he, or she, mean by making her pay the price?

But what chilled Kate the most, more than the fact that someone might be following her movements, were the last few words: *and the others before her.*

If Wary Watcher was Lily's killer, was he saying

that he had killed other people too? Was Kate going to discover a trail of bodies? What had she gotten herself into?

She reached for her phone to call Mack at the same time a chime sounded and she jumped, knocking the Pop-Tart she'd barely eaten to the floor and sending a flurry of crumbs scattering across the hardwood surface. Her phone chimed again, alerting her to an incoming text from Mack. I have something I want to run by you. Care to grab a bite to eat?

Sure. Where do you want to meet? She could tell him about Wary Watcher in person, and he'd undoubtedly reassure her that he was just some internet jerk. Kate started scooping the Pop-Tart crumbs up, then thought better of that plan. "Hey, Harley! I have a treat for you." The dog came bounding in, scrambled under the desk and began making quick work of the mess.

Skyview Diner, Mack wrote. I think we should both get a sense of the place at night.

For a second, she had thought he was asking her on a date. Dinner at the Italian place just out of Fordham or a sunset picnic in the park. The Skyview Diner meant this was a working meeting, not a date. She told herself that was good, because she'd keep her focus on finding Lily, not finding out how Mack felt about her. Give me twenty minutes, she texted back.

She was scheduled to record the next episode tonight, but she could delay dropping that one for a few hours. If Mack had information she could use on the show, then that took priority over taping the episode. All she wanted was more information, and yet, she found herself touching up her makeup, letting her hair down from its usual ponytail and changing into a pale pink sweater. Anticipation to see him had her hurrying out the door and, once again, arriving several minutes early.

She could see Mack already inside, seated at a booth by a window. There was a chill in the air, and when she opened the door to the Skyview Diner, the cold air whooshed right in behind her. Mack's black leather jacket served as a stark contrast to the pale blue polo shirt he was wearing. He flashed her a smile that made Kate feel welcome, safe and happy all at the same time.

She slid into the opposite seat of the booth and shrugged out of her jacket. A waitress came by and Kate ordered a hot tea. "It's chilly out tonight."

"Which is why I have coffee." He raised his cup in her direction. "That and for the caffeine."

"Putting in long days?"

"When am I not?" He chuckled, then sobered. The waitress came by with a small pot of hot water, a mug and a selection of tea bags. Mack waited until she left before speaking again. "I have something to share with you that we need to keep between us only. No podcast, no talking to the neighbors about it. Just you and me."

"But—"

"No buts about it. What I'm about to tell you cannot leave this table. It could cost me my job. My chief directly ordered me to stop working these cases, but I know there's something wrong here. I can't let someone get away with hurting someone else again, not on my watch."

She stopped protesting because she got the sense that this had all become very personal for Mack in the last couple of days. As much as she wanted to get the word out about Lily, her priorities had shifted. Protecting Mack, and anyone else who was caught in this, came first. For a long time, she'd put the podcast ahead of people, which had created that disaster last summer. No more. The people she cared about were the ones who had to be her priority, and she knew in that moment that Mack was one of those people.

"I appreciate you trusting me, Mack, and I hope you know that whatever we talk about will be kept between us." Kate dipped her tea bag into the hot water a couple more times, then set it on the saucer. "You said investigations plural. You're looking at more than just Lily?"

"What you told me about Elaine's autopsy got me thinking. I told you something was nagging at me with that information, right?"

She nodded. "And I had the same feeling."

"Well, that feeling turned out to be spot-on." He withdrew two sheets of paper from his inside pocket, unfolded them and placed them on the table between them. "This is Elaine's autopsy report, and this is Luke's." Then he shook his head and put a hand over the papers, blocking her view. "I'm sorry. I didn't think. If this is too hard for you to look at—"

How thoughtful of Mack to consider her feelings and her grief. Maybe she was becoming one of those people he cared about too. "It's fine. I've seen his autopsy report. When I started the podcast, I requested the case files under FOIA. I didn't look at the crime scene photos, because that was just too much to bear, but I did read all the reports."

"Maybe that's why you had the same feeling I did." He moved his hand and pointed to the sketch of the body on each of the reports. "Both Luke and Elaine were shot in the same place." He moved his finger down to the notes at the bottom of the sheet. "And with the same caliber bullet."

"They never found a gun at Wheatly's house, or by Luke's body or beside Elaine." The theory had been that the killer left the scene with the gun that had killed Luke, and Elaine's gun had tumbled into the creek and been whisked away by the rushing water that had built up after a summer storm. That had been the explanation for the lack of evidence on her hands and clothing, and the missing bullet and shell casing too.

"I know."

"Wheatly did carry guns, because he was a hunter, and he had a history of criminal activity involving a weapon," Kate said. "He could have learned from his past mistakes and thrown the gun away to get rid of the evidence. That's what the prosecutor said."

"Then why does Elaine have almost exactly the same fatal wound, in almost exactly the same place, with exactly the same kind of bullet? Elaine's was a through-and-through wound, and the bullet was never recovered. She was there a long time before they found her. Anything could have happened to that evidence." Mack tapped the sketch of Elaine's skull. "Either way, it couldn't have been Wheatly who shot her because he was in prison already."

"So Luke is murdered, and then Lily disappears soon after that. It's several months before Wheatly is arrested and prosecuted. But while he's in prison, Elaine disappears too. That's three crimes or cases or whatever you want to call them in a relatively short period of time, in a small town that rarely has anything more than noise complaints. Maybe it is a coincidence because they don't all tie to one person—because that person was in jail at the time."

"Do you know what my dad used to call coincidence?" Mack folded the papers back into thirds and tucked them inside his jacket again. "Evidence."

The information spun in Kate's head, details that couldn't possibly add up. "Either way, none of this has anything to do with Lily, right? Except the fact that Luke and Elaine both knew her, their cases are all different, and there doesn't seem to be another person in common with what happened to all of them."

"Maybe not. But I think it speaks to a bigger problem." His gaze went to somewhere far away, and grief seemed to weigh down his shoulders. "My father was either incompetent or purposely not doing his job well."

"Oh, come on, Mack. Your dad was difficult to

deal with and, yes, could have worked harder on Luke's case, but that sounds like a pretty serious accusation to me."

"Which is why this has to stay between us. I don't know what to think or how to look at this information. I just needed your opinion and…" He crossed his hands on the table. "Your advice."

The idea that Mack wanted to lean on her warmed Kate's heart. It had been a long time since she opened her heart to another person, and had that person open theirs too. She'd grown to really like Mack, to look forward to seeing him and to appreciate his intelligence and the way he challenged her. Now she was seeing a vulnerable side, something she suspected he rarely showed. "I don't know how I can advise you. If anything, you've been the shoulder I've been leaning on. I went into this podcast thinking I knew what I was doing, but you've been smart and supportive and tactical throughout this whole thing."

He smiled. "I appreciate that, but I'm truly just doing my job."

"Oh. Yeah." She masked her disappointment at him equating their time together as just his job and reminded herself that Lily was the priority. Whatever warm feelings she was having weren't being reciprocated. "How can I help?"

"If I pursue this evidence, I will lose my job. The chief has made that abundantly clear. I will also very likely destroy any relationship I have with my father. I have a stack of reports and investigations sitting on my desk that need my attention. But I feel this urge…

no, more like a need, to follow these cases through. To dive deep and make sure what I'm seeing is nothing more than a lot of common factors." He sighed. "Yet, if I do that, I'm hurting my job and my father."

How she could relate to that. She'd had the same mental battle when she launched her podcast. "When I first started the podcast, I felt guilty. I was spending all this time looking into Luke's murder. Time I wasn't spending with my dad, not that our relationship was all that great, time I wasn't spending with my friends, with Luke's dog or with myself so that I could grieve. The coffee shop had been struggling ever since I took it over, and if I put too much time into the podcast, I could lose the shop and my mother's dream."

"How did you balance it? How did you decide where to put your energies?"

"Every time I got to a crossroads, I sat down and prayed. I asked God for guidance. And if I was quiet long enough, He answered me."

Mack scoffed. "It's been a long time since I prayed like that."

"Well, maybe it's time you started, Detective." She gave him a smile, then slid out of the booth. "I've got to go home and record my episode. I have to release it tomorrow. Don't worry—none of what you told me tonight will be on the air. I'm going to run Ashley's interview."

"Thank you, Kate. You're a good woman."

She wanted to believe he'd said that because he liked her, because he might be feeling the same closeness she was. It was only a few seconds ago that he'd reminded her this was all about work, not about them. She'd do well to keep her heart protected from falling any further.

"Nah. I'm just trying to do my job." She gave the table a light tap. "Have a good night, Detective."

Chapter Eleven

The last time Mack Snyder prayed had been when he was eleven. His grandmother, the kindest person he had ever known, had a sudden stroke and died just hours before her seventieth birthday party. He'd been so mad at God that day for taking one of his favorite people away, for yanking her out of his life with no warning, and leaving nothing to ease the sudden, gaping hole. Over the years, he'd drifted away from religion and church, but it had always been there, on the periphery of his thoughts and his life.

Then along came Kate McAllister, the last person in the world he would have thought could stand in his corner and give him the motivation to get close to God again. He wasn't sure he knew how to do that, or whether or not God even wanted to hear from a long-lost son.

Mack's house was quiet, with nothing but the ticking of the kitchen clock to keep him company. He unloaded his gun and his belt, then crossed to the bench under the living room window. The town of Fordham had gone to sleep, most of the houses dark, with only the streetlights dotting the landscape like fireflies against the dark background of the mountains. He dropped to his knees and, for a moment, had no idea what to say.

Just have a conversation with the Big Guy, his grandmother used to say on the dozens of nights he'd stayed at her house while his parents were working. She'd tuck him into bed with a glass of milk, a warm hug and a reminder to say his prayers. *He doesn't need all that formality.*

Mack bowed his head and crossed his hands before him. "God, I know it's been a while. Okay, a long while. I don't even know what to say. I just need…some direction. Show me where you want me to go, and I'll go. I—"

His phone rang, the insistent, loud tone of the police department, a clear reminder that his job didn't care about anything other than his immediate attention. Mack knew, however, that a call after hours from the department meant nothing good. Prayer would have to wait. He scrambled to get the phone out of his pocket. "Snyder."

"Detective, we found a body," the desk sergeant said. "You're going to want to come down right now."

There was little left of Lily Ridge after three years, but there was no mistaking the purple sweatshirt and dark purple sneakers the officers found buried in the shallow grave. Mack stood over the spot where Lily's skeleton had been found by a hunter and said a silent prayer for the young girl who hadn't been a runaway after all. She'd barely made it to the edge of town and had been found less than a mile from where her car had been left. A mere three miles from her home.

The Fordham Police Department, inexperienced in murders and bodies that had been left in the woods for years, had called in a crime scene unit from the NCSBI, the North Carolina State Bureau of Investigation, to process the ground and search for all the tiny bones that were scattered about the site. Mack had stayed there for hours, watching the evidence techs do their job. The case was no longer his; once the NCSBI came in, they were the lead on the case. He lingered, not because he was needed on the scene, but because he wanted to make sure Lily was taken care of, respected, and had someone there who was at least familiar with her. He owed the family that much. And a whole lot more.

"Detective, you should see this." One of the NCSBI officers waved him over to the stretcher sitting by the coroner's truck. Lily's skeletal remains had been placed in a body bag, laid out in order to the best of the officers' ability. At the top of the bed sat her skull, so starkly pale against the dark plastic bag. A fractured hole at the top of her skull peered straight into a gaping hole that had taken out a large portion of the back of her skull.

"Is that a gunshot wound?" Mack asked.

"Yes. Looks like maybe a .45 or a .38 caliber.

Hard to tell without measuring." The officer zipped the body bag shut, then signaled to the coroner's assistant that he could take the remains to the morgue. "We'll have a report for you in a couple of days, but preliminaries say she was shot on the left side of the temple and died pretty instantly from that wound."

Shot on the left side of the temple. Just like Elaine. Just like Luke. This was beginning to look an awful lot like a pattern, although that made no sense. "Are you sure about that?"

The tech shrugged. "Like I said, we won't know for sure until we complete the autopsy, and if we get damned lucky and find a casing or bullet. It's been a long time, so chances are not good. Anyway, we'll be in touch."

The evidence techs began to pack up their gear and load the trucks. They shut down the bright lights that had covered the space, plunging it into near darkness. A full moon sat overhead, like a single eye watching the tragedy below.

"Detective?" the tech said. "We're done here. You can go home if you want."

Mack stared at the mound of earth that had just been combed through for the bones of a little girl who was never going home. It seemed disrespectful to leave the spot without having a moment to honor and memorialize Lily Ridge. "Just give me a minute, will you?"

"Sure thing." The NCSBI team left, two of the vans heading for headquarters and the third turning toward the morgue.

Mack stood outside the ring of yellow crime scene tape for a long time. An owl hooted as darkness blanketed over the woods. And still Mack stayed and whispered silent prayers that were much too late.

Kate woke up very early the next morning with a feeling of dread hanging over her shoulders. Harley was in his usual spot at the foot of the bed, snoring away, and the house was quiet. Still, something was off. No, something was *wrong*. She picked up her phone and saw two missed calls from Mack that came in while she was sleeping, and a text that said simply, Call me right away, no matter what time it is.

The phone seemed to ring forever before Mack answered. It was only five-thirty in the morning, but his voice sounded strong and awake. "Kate. Thank God you called."

"They found her, didn't they?" There was only one thing that would have Mack up that early and trying to reach her in the middle of the night. Kate's heart stopped in the space before he answered, and a part of her prayed he would say the call had nothing to do with Lily. As much as Kate wanted answers, she wanted to bring Lily home, intact and alive, even more.

Then Mack let out a long, heavy sigh, and Kate's heart fractured. "Yes. In the woods about a mile from where her car was found."

"And she was dead?" Even as Kate asked the question, some insane glimmer of hope stubbornly tried to rise in her chest. Maybe she'd been coming back home from Florida, maybe she'd been living in one of those remote cabins along the mountainside, maybe—

"Yes. I'm sorry."

A wave of grief nearly as strong as the one that had hit her after Luke died rolled in like a tsunami. Lily wasn't living in some shack in Panama City Beach. She wasn't in that city because she'd fallen in love with some guy years ago. She was dead, and every worst fear her mother had ever had was coming true. No one had found her in time. No one had stopped this monster from plucking Lily from the earth.

"If it's any consolation, they think it was quick," Mack said. "No one can say for sure until they do the autopsy, but I don't think she suffered."

"Thank God." That stubborn glimmer of hope wriggled to the forefront once again, because maybe they were wrong, maybe they had jumped to conclusions, and she asked, "But…are you sure it was Lily?"

Mack described the purple sneakers they had found and the purple sweatshirt that had been in the shallow grave. Exactly the clothing Lily's mom had told the police her daughter was wearing.

And then Kate knew, and believed, and everything she had feared suddenly became a reality. A sharp pain tore her chest. Her legs threatened to buckle. "It's really her?"

Mack's voice was soft and low. "I'm sorry. I just got home from telling her parents and it was…

heart-wrenching. There are no words anyone can say to parents who have been through that kind of tragedy."

"I feel so horrible for them. They kept on hoping, as we all did, that she would come home." Kate sighed. "Do you think…you could show me where they found her?" She needed to see with her own eyes, just as she had with Luke. Maybe it was part of accepting what had happened, or maybe it was just a masochistic tendency, but Kate had to know.

"I don't think that's a good idea, Kate. It's a crime scene right now."

"But they've already removed all the evidence, right?" She didn't mention that the media had probably already descended on the spot like hungry vultures. Then she realized she was one of those vultures. Was her quest for closure justification for going to the site? For asking a favor of Mack that no one else could ask?

She searched her heart. How pure were her motives? Was it still about Lily, or partly about reporting on the scene for the podcast? She didn't know, and that didn't sit well with her conscience.

"I understand you wanting to go," he said. "To be honest, I had a hard time leaving last night. Even though her body is no longer there, I felt like she shouldn't be alone. It doesn't make any sense because she's not there in any way, shape or form anymore."

"It makes perfect sense, Mack. Why don't I meet you and we go there for a few minutes and just honor Lily?" Kate said, resolving in that moment that she wasn't going to record a report at the crime scene. She would take no photos. She would simply be there and remember Lily as she was, before. "I'm not going for the story, in case you're worried about that. I'm going for me, for her family and, most of all, for her."

"I'm sitting in my car on the side of the road because I had to come back here after I saw her parents. I just couldn't leave her. Not yet." Mack rattled off directions to Kate. "I'll wait here for you."

"Thank you." She hung up the phone, then hurried to get out of bed, throw on some jeans and hiking boots then swoop her hair into a ponytail. She texted Jeremy to say she wouldn't be in that morning, then got in her car.

When she pulled up behind Mack, he was already outside his car, leaning on the hood. Kate walked over to him and handed him a thermos. "It's fresh brewed but from my pot at home, so it's not as good as what I have at the shop."

He gave her a tired smile. "You read my mind. I ran out of coffee hours ago, and I'm too old to be up all night."

She laughed but stopped herself. The sound seemed so wrong when something so horrible had happened just a few hundred yards away. And yet, the birds were still singing, the trees rustling in the breeze and the sun was inching higher in the sky, waking the flowers and animals from their slumber. It all seemed so normal, so beautiful and, most of all, so odd. Laughing or even enjoying the warmth of the spring sun on her face seemed inappropriate somehow.

Mack put a hand on her shoulder. "I didn't know Lily, but I've read and heard a lot about her. What I know tells me she wouldn't want anyone to be sad for too long just because she was gone."

"You're right. But it's still hard." Mack nodded, then started moving, trudging into the woods and down the hill. Kate fell into step behind him.

The dense trees and foliage gave way to a small patch where sunlight struggled to get past the leaf cover. A log sat against the trunk of one tree, with a massive pile of leaves stacked behind it. To the right was a bare patch where the grass, shrubs and rocks had been removed. The oval shape of a shallow grave remained, stark and dark against the lush green forest. This was where Lily had lain for three years, alone, while her mother grieved and the police gave up. It infuriated Kate that any of this had to happen. If James Snyder had done his job correctly, Lily would have surely been found much sooner.

Mack, however, wasn't James. Mack was trying to help her, and she could see his own heartbreak and somber acceptance.

"Poor Lily. I'm so sorry she ended up here and it took so long to find her." Kate picked her way down the slope with Mack, stopping just at the edge of the yellow tape. Emotions rumbled through her, and she fought to hold back the tears that threatened to fall. Mack stood silently beside her, his tall, broad strength a comfort and support.

"There's nothing more we can do," he said after a while. "The NCSBI has the case, and this site is just woods again. She's gone, Kate, in every sense of the word."

Kate turned to him. "We can tell her story, and we can find who did this."

"NCSBI took the reins, so we can't. Fordham doesn't really have a lot of experience with this kind of thing, so I thought it best to call in NCSBI."

"That doesn't mean you stop investigating here, Mack. You can still—"

"It means exactly that, Kate. They're in charge. If I go off on my own investigation, I'm disobeying orders. I could get fired for that. Listen, NCSBI knows what they're doing. They have the technology and the experts to process this and find the evidence to put this guy in jail for a long time."

She spun away instead of shouting at him. Frustration bubbled inside her chest. She understood his reasoning for calling in the state, but doing so had left Mack's hands tied, which also left her without his resources and help. Just when they were beginning to get somewhere with Lily's case, he'd essentially hamstrung them both. The NCSBI would do their job, of that she was sure, but they were not going to keep Mack or Kate in the loop.

Kate picked her way through the brush outside the crime scene tape. Mack stayed behind, sipping his coffee and staring at the space where Lily's skeletal remains had been found. Nervous energy propelled

Kate forward, in a widening circle that skirted the yellow perimeter.

She stumbled over a branch that was buried under some leaves and nearly hit the ground. Her palms broke her fall, but slid against the slippery leaves. As she scrambled back to her feet, a flash of something silver caught her eye. A metal corner on a small rectangular object peeked out from beneath the pile of leaves she had disturbed when she fell. Kate grabbed a stick, then nudged the leaves aside.

The long slim metal body of a lighter glinted in the early morning sun. It was one of those old-fashioned ones, thick and heavy and monogrammed. She'd seen that lighter before, in a photo, back when she was researching Luke's case and had dug up everything she could find about his murderer.

Three ornate letters covered the face of the lighter, and changed everything Kate thought she knew about the Lily Ridge case: *JDW*.

John David Wheatly. But that was impossible. Wasn't it?

Chapter Twelve

The NCSBI descended once again, this time widening their grid search. Ultimately, the lighter was the only piece of real evidence they found. After three years and a lot of animal and nature activity, there wasn't much else to find anyway. They'd found most of Lily's bones but not all of them, a tragedy that Mack would never tell the family. A tech bagged and tagged the lighter, then thanked Mack for alerting them to the find.

Kate had gone back to work at Mack's insistence, protesting the whole way. Mack lingered at the woods, then finally got in his car and headed home. All the while, he replayed the early morning stop at the Ridge home.

It had been barely five in the morning when he'd gone there. Grace Ridge was an early riser, something he knew from her emails to him over the years. She had opened the door before he even knocked, and when she saw him, she took a step back, her hand over her mouth, her eyes filling with tears. "We found your daughter," he said, "and I'm deeply sorry to say she died, probably right after she went missing."

Grace had been stoic for a long time after hearing those horrible words, then she began to slowly collapse into her grief. First her shoulders fell, then her knees crumpled and she reached out, flailing, lost. Mack took her hands in his, then helped her into a chair. He hurried into the kitchen and poured her a glass of water because he had no idea what else to do. He'd never had to do a death notification before, and doing this one, for a case he'd been so close to, made him feel horrible.

"Thank you, Detective," Grace said. She set the water on a small table but didn't drink. Tears rolled down her face in skinny silent rivers.

"There is no need to thank me, ma'am. I'm sorry that this is the news I have to deliver."

"I appreciate you making the visit in person." Grace drew her knees up to her chest and held them tight. Resignation weighed down her words. "I guess I always knew she was dead. My Lily never would have left without a word. But you coming here closed that door of hope, and maybe that's a good thing because now I can at least move on."

He didn't know what to say or how to comfort her. Mack had never been especially good in these kinds of situations. All he could do was his job. "I want you to know we will be reopening the investigation."

"It's about time, Detective. Your father did a terri-

ble job of looking into my daughter's disappearance."
She leaned forward until their gazes met. "And I
think you should ask him why."

Mack couldn't argue back or defend his father
because the truth was, Grace was right. James had
done a terrible job on this case, as he had with the
two before it. The question was why, and what that
said about the Snyder legacy. "We will be looking
into everything. This is the NCSBI's case now, but
I know they would like to interview you again in a
few days, or whenever you are comfortable coming
in to talk to them. This might be a hard time."

"Detective, the last three years have been hard.
Now?" She straightened in the chair and seemed to
gain some kind of inner steel. "Now I have an answer, and I can put one foot in front of the other and
bury my daughter. I can come in to talk to them tomorrow if that works."

Mack had texted the lead detective from the
NCSBI and coordinated a time for Grace's interview.
In between, Mack apologized another half dozen
times and still felt like he could have said he was
sorry a hundred more times and it still wouldn't be
enough. When he left, he heard the soft click of the
door behind him, then the heartbreaking sound of
Grace Ridge sobbing.

Mack spent a couple restless hours in his apartment, trying to nap and instead pacing the small
rooms. His mind whirled with all of the information
he'd gathered in the last few days, the jigsaw puzzle
that was beginning to become clear. Grace Ridge

finally had some answers—even if they weren't the ones she wanted—and maybe it was high time Mack got some of his own.

It was just after nine when he pulled into the driveway. His father wasn't working in the yard today. Instead, he was in the garage, under the hood of his car, changing out the spark plugs. Like the rest of the house, James's garage was so pristine, it seemed as if the grease didn't dare smudge on the floor. Pictures of his father hunting, camping and hiking hung on the walls, a collage of memories he had with his friends. James was a man's man, the kind who manned the grill and popped a beer at the end of the day, who rooted for the Pats and booed the Eagles. Who would go to the ends of the earth to help a friend in need—

But had little use for his own children. There wasn't a single picture with Mack or Rachel, no memories of outdoorsy things with either of them. His father had preferred to do those kinds of things with "the boys," leaving the kids with their mother most weekends. Maybe that was part of why Mack tried so hard to get his father's attention and to force his father to see Mack as a man too.

When Mack entered the garage, his father straightened, then grabbed a rag to wipe the grease off his hands. "Well, well. Two visits in a week. Are you sure it isn't Christmas?"

Mack scowled at the sarcasm in his father's voice. "You complain when I don't come by and complain when I do."

"I'd just appreciate a son with some dependability, that's all."

The dig made Mack bristle, but he brushed it off. Undoubtedly there would be more statements like that from his father, and if he let James's words get his hackles up already, he'd accomplish nothing in this visit. "You got a minute to talk, Dad?"

"I guess so. I was going to have some breakfast anyway." He folded the rag and laid it on the workbench before leading the way into the house.

The garage door opened into a small, tidy kitchen. There were no dishes in the sink, no crumbs on the counter, no mail left unopened. Everything was categorized, organized and stored in its proper place. His father washed his hands, then dried both his hands and the sink after he was through.

"Well, I don't have all day," his father said. "Why are you here?"

Mack had thought about all the ways he could come at this conversation on the way over. Direct confrontation was never a good idea with his father, who would take it as an attack. "We found Lily Ridge, about a mile from where her car was found. She'd been shot in the head."

"Wow. That's too bad." His voice held all the emotion of a can of paint.

"What's too bad is that we spent three years thinking she was a runaway." Frustration rose in his throat, and try as he might, he couldn't keep it from bleeding into his words. Every time he thought of how much and how long Grace Ridge had suffered and agonized, it made Mack angry. "We might have been able to find her sooner if the case hadn't been closed."

"Are you criticizing my work?" James slid a cup of coffee across the table. Mack took a seat while his father leaned against the kitchen counter and sipped at his mug.

"I'm just wondering why you ignored evidence." Okay, so direct confrontation it was. Mack could feel the conversation going sideways, but he couldn't seem to stop himself. "Her best friend, Ashley, said some creepy guy had been stalking her. There's no witness statement to that effect in Lily's case file. In fact, Ashley's statement is barely a paragraph."

"That's because the girl didn't have much to say. You know teenagers. They keep their mouths shut around adults." His father shrugged, nonplussed. "If she's talking about some creepy guy, this is the first I've heard of it."

How did his father not feel the same frustration that Mack did? How could he treat the murder of a teenage girl with such detachment? This super detective who'd been honored by the town more than once had to have cared at some point. Or had that all been a sham? "This isn't the first case where you haven't exactly been on top of the evidence, Dad."

Anger sparked in his father's eyes and sharpened his tone. "Are you telling me I didn't do my job? You have barely twenty-four months of experience, and I have thirty *years*. You don't know what you're talking about."

All the other times Mack had come across this side of his father, he had chosen to back down. His father had, as he said, more experience, more knowledge, more everything, and Mack had lived in that massive shadow all his life, questioning his every move, every decision. He had deferred to his father, tried to impress his father and longed to be like his father. But as Mack had unraveled the case of Lily Ridge, he'd realized that the shadow his father cast was all a sham, and he was tired of pretending it was anything else.

This time, a girl had been murdered and a woman was falling to pieces on the other side of her front door because James Snyder didn't follow the trail. "I know more than you think I do, Dad. I know that a sixteen-year-old girl is being buried because no one went looking for her. I know that this girl was killed the same way Luke Winslow was and that there was evidence at the scene linking a man who was already in jail to Lily's murder."

"You talking about Wheatly?" His father waved that off like it was a fly buzzing around his head. "He's a waste of space. Don't let him fool you into thinking he's anything other than an attention hound claiming involvement in something he had nothing to do with."

"Then why was his lighter found near Lily's remains?"

James froze. His face paled. For a second, he didn't say anything, then he seemed to recover and wipe the shock from his features. "Wheatly was a hunter. Probably dropped it out there one day. Coincidence, nothing more."

Mack's coffee had gone cold. He'd never even taken a sip, and he didn't care. "What have you always told me a coincidence in a case is? Evidence, Dad. Evidence."

"There is no evidence there." His father's words were even, pointed, tinted with anger. "Wheatly lived in those mountains. He was like a billy goat, climbing all over them every day. Come talk to me when you have something real."

"This is real evidence, Dad. The lighter is engraved with his initials, and there is a photo online with him holding it, so there's no question that it was his. What I want to know is how it ended up beside Lily Ridge's body." Mack got to his feet. He knew he was pushing his luck, because he could see his father shutting down, the wall going up between them. James was like a cornered dog who would never concede, only fight his way out of the situation. Maybe it was the tragedy of seeing Lily's remains, of the starkness of that purple sweatshirt buried deep in the woods, but Mack couldn't stop asking the questions. "And one more thing. Why were Luke Winslow, Elaine Reynolds and Lily Ridge all shot in the same place, and how did you not notice that when you looked at their autopsies?"

"Elaine Reynolds? That one was a suicide. Don't you have enough work to do? Is that why you're opening up cases that have been closed for years?" His father turned away and began rustling in the cabinet for some bread. He put two slices into the toaster and pressed the button. "You should be doing your job."

"I *am* doing my job."

"Seems to me like you don't know what you're doing. At all. Nor do you have any sense of family loyalty. If you truly wanted to make me proud, you'd stop digging into things you have no cause to be digging into. All you're doing is making me look bad. Forget it. I'm done with this conversation and with you." His father left the toast behind and stalked out of the kitchen. "You can see yourself out."

"I'll do exactly that," Mack said under his breath.

Ashley's second interview was teary and full of regret, but she did manage to paint a vivid picture of what Lily had been like when she was alive. They talked about the tragedy of Lily's death, and plans for a memorial to celebrate Lily's life. Kate added some snippets from other interviews she had done, then promised her listeners a big update once the autopsy results were back.

"Thank you all for listening and for commenting on the Facebook page. I appreciate your efforts to help me find her. I know we wanted to bring her home alive, but Lily is home now, and that's what matters. Until next time, be safe, listeners." She clicked off the mic, finished off the recording and then dropped the episode. In a few hours, the social media page for the podcast would be abuzz with comments, but right now, Kate barely cared. Seeing where Lily had been found had sapped her emotional energy and left her feeling…empty.

Jenn was curled up on the couch when Kate emerged from her office. "You doing okay?"

"Yeah. Sort of." She dropped onto the couch, tucked her legs underneath herself and let out a long breath. She'd held it together throughout the podcast, but now, the mountain of emotions in her heart weighed a thousand pounds. "It's like Luke dying all over again. The evidence, the investigation, the aftermath. And then Elaine and now… Lily. I went to see Grace today, and the grief in her face reminded me of what it was like when Luke died. I cried, she cried and it was just so…sad and tragic."

Jenn drew her into a hug. "I'm sorry. I can only imagine how hard this is for you."

Kate leaned into Jenn's support, into that safe space for all the feelings whirling inside her. It wasn't grieving Luke so much as it was grieving the loss of so many good people who never should have died. Someone had senselessly hurt Luke, Lily and maybe even Elaine, and unless they figured out who that was, he would hurt someone else. He had to be stopped, but it seemed as if all her efforts to change the tides were a waste.

Maybe the podcast she had started with such high hopes of bringing closure and justice to other people's stories wasn't doing what she'd prayed it would. Maybe she had no business trying to fix what was already broken, especially while a part of her was still broken too.

She and Jenn talked for a long time, until Kate started to yawn and Jenn said they both needed to get some sleep. Kate lay in her bed for a long time, but her mind kept whirring. Finally, she got out of bed, booted up her laptop and went to the show's social media page. Just seeing all those names of people who were as invested as Kate was made her feel better. Lily would not be forgotten. There were hundreds of people mourning right alongside Grace Ridge, and Kate and so many others.

Then Kate's gaze caught on a familiar handle. Wary Watcher had posted under the show notes for today's episode. His was one of dozens of comments, buried amid a flurry of theories and support. She realized then that after everything that had happened, she hadn't mentioned Wary Watcher's last post to Mack. She'd gone and made that stupid comment back to him, thinking she had called him out, but his reply said otherwise.

You're never going to catch me because you're looking in the wrong spot. Lily won't be the last, and she wasn't the first.

The blood in Kate's veins went cold. She drew her blankets up around her, and held them tight, but her skin refused to warm. She stared at the comment, and for the first time since she began the podcast, Kate was afraid.

Chapter Thirteen

The NCSBI had made it very clear that Mack was not to interfere in the Lily Ridge investigation. They'd dusted Wheatly's lighter for fingerprints and found three clear prints that matched the ones they already had on file for Wheatly. The lead detective, however, told Mack to stay out of his investigation and sent Mack on his way.

For the rest of the morning, Mack typed up paperwork, filed statements and made calls about stolen lawn mowers and missing planters. At three, he'd had enough and decided if NCSBI wasn't going to let him be a part of the investigation, he'd start one of his own because there was no way he could let another case be brushed under the rug. He'd be disobeying orders and risking his job, but he was tired of playing by the rules when the people he had trusted to do their jobs had let him down.

Kate was just locking up the coffee shop when Mack pulled up. He rolled down the window and gave his horn a tap. She jumped a mile high and pressed a hand to her chest. "You scared me! What is wrong with you?"

"Sorry." Had her reaction seemed a little over-the-top? She'd looked terrified there for a second. Then he dismissed the concerns. He was just blowing her reaction out of proportion. "You feel like breaking the rules a little bit?"

A mischievous, excited grin curved across her face. "Is it a day that ends in *Y*?"

He unlocked the passenger's side door for her. He loved that Kate was adventurous and up for about anything. She trusted him, too, and clearly admired the work he did. They made a good team, balancing each other out with caution and spontaneity, and Mack liked that. A lot. "Then get in and let's go do a little detective work of our own."

"Where are we going?" she asked as he pulled out of the parking space and started heading down Main Street. The sun was high in the sky, warming the streets of Fordham. Later, when the sun went down, the warm days of spring would yield to cool, mountain temps. But for now, it was pleasant and sunny, like a spring day anywhere. The beautiful weather made it seem wrong to be investigating murder.

"I want to know why Wheatly's lighter was in the woods," Mack said. "I would have asked him myself but Piedmont wouldn't let me in to see him today. The warden said they had a situation going up there, which probably means there's been a murder in the prison. They told me to come by tomorrow. In the meantime, I want to…" Mack flicked a glance in her direction, gauging how she might respond. "Well, I want to look inside his house."

She arched a brow and a smile curved one side of her face. "Are we breaking and entering, Detective Snyder?"

"Don't get too excited. The city owns his house because he didn't pay his taxes the last few years. They haven't auctioned it off yet, but it's scheduled to go on the block at the end of summer. Until then, it's technically the property of Fordham."

"And thus, under the jurisdiction of the police department."

"In a very loose definition of the word, yes. Technically, I can be on the property but you'll be trespassing."

"Good thing I know a cop who probably won't arrest me." She chuckled. They passed the last shop on Main Street and headed out of town, climbing toward the mountains. "What are we looking for when we get there?"

"Frankly, I don't know. Like I said, that lighter bothers me, and until I can figure out why and how it got there, I'm going to keep digging."

Wheatly had never mentioned anything about Lily until the day they went to see him. *I will tell you that when you find that girl, you'll know it wasn't me what killed the Winslow guy, or anyone else.*

What did Wheatly mean? And what did it have to do with Luke's death?

The drive to Wheatly's house wound through hilly

backroads and up a heavily wooded mountainside. The closer they got to the small ramshackle cabin in the woods, the less the sun beamed through the dense foliage and the more ominous the air became. Even Kate was silent beside him, her posture tense and nervous.

The paved road yielded to a dirt road that spilled out into a yard that was more weeds than grass. Several rusted-out cars were being overtaken by weeds and trees. The roof on the one-bedroom cabin was missing several shingles, and it sagged over the porch like a frown. The white lid of a dented, rusty chest freezer sat against the front of the empty container, probably raided by a bear long ago. Mack thought of Kate sitting in this very driveway three years ago, trying to catch a killer herself after months of the police doing virtually nothing. The place was so desolate, it sent a chill up his spine to think about what could have happened if the police hadn't arrived quickly.

"You ready?" Mack asked.

"It's weird being back here." She stared out the windshield and seemed to shiver. He wondered what she was thinking, then realized it was probably the same thought he'd had. *But for the grace of God...* "Yes, I'm ready."

The front door stood ajar, with a pile of leaves trailing from the porch and into the dark house. Mack switched on his flashlight. "Wait here while I clear the house."

She gave him a look of disbelief. "Mack, no one is living here."

"Doesn't mean there aren't any creatures in here or that a homeless person isn't staying here. That happens more often than you think, especially when you're this far from civilization—and police." He unclipped his gun, flicked off the safety and raised it to eye level. "I'll be right back." He made his way through the house in less than a minute. The cabin was two rooms and a bathroom. The main room served as a kitchen/dining/living space all in one and had a bare minimum of furniture. A battered leather recliner faced an old TV that weighed at least a hundred pounds and was flanked by an aluminum folding tray. One broken kitchen chair sat against the wall, and another was tucked beneath a small gateleg table.

The bedroom held a stained full-size mattress topped by a tangle of sheets, a small dresser with a broken drawer and a plastic basket of clothes. A few hangers hung in the closet, but it didn't look like Wheatly ever wore much other than jeans and T-shirts. The bathroom was barely big enough to hold a toilet and a stand-up shower, with water that came from a well out back.

There were few cobwebs, and except for the leaves by the front door, Mother Nature had barely intruded in the house. It looked like Wheatly had just left for the weekend, not for the rest of his life.

"It's empty," he called to Kate. "Not much in here to begin with anyway."

Kate did a slow turn in the living space. "What do you think we're going to find here?"

"Maybe nothing. But we have to look just in case." Ever since he'd found the lighter, he'd had the urge to look into Wheatly more closely.

They each put on a pair of latex gloves, then started going through cabinets in the kitchen, before searching the drawers. Wheatly had a few plates and pans, and only a handful of silverware. Mack found a couple cans of soup and a can of beans, both relatively new. Seemed odd, but maybe a hitchhiker had crashed here for a few nights. There was no other sign anyone was here or had been for a long time.

"He lived pretty light," Kate said. "I don't think he went into town much, either."

"Wheatly hunted and probably got most of his meals from the woods right here. We know he had a couple rifles and a .38 that he kept with him pretty much all the time." Mack thumbed toward the other room. "There's a dresser and a closet in the bedroom. Let's search those."

Kate started with the dresser, while Mack checked the closet. He tugged at the carpet, looking for a secret hideaway place, but it didn't budge. There were no false panels in the walls, nothing that seemed to hold any personal possessions. Mack rose on his tiptoes and patted the high shelf. A plume of dust burst into his face. He started coughing, and as he bent to avoid the next cloud, his hand hit something cardboard. "Hey, Kate? I think I found something."

He pulled a cigar box out of the closet. It was covered with dust and so faded he could barely read the brand. Kate yanked up the shade in the bedroom, filling the space with bright afternoon sun. Mack sat on the bed and opened the lid.

A rubber band held a stack of pictures together. Those sat atop a couple of Christmas cards from Wheatly's mother and stepfather. He had a few stray keys in the box and a birth announcement for a nephew. Mack twisted off the rubber band and started flipping through the photos. Kate perched on the edge of the bed beside him and watched over his shoulder.

The first few pictures were of Wheatly as a child. A typical kid living in the North Carolina mountains, playing in the dirt, swimming in the lake. There was a picture of his mother, then a much later one with her second husband, who Mack had heard was a mean man who had given Wheatly his surname and not much else.

As Mack reached the last photo, he opened his mouth to tell Kate the whole idea had been a bust. Then he saw a familiar face standing beside two other men, all three of them dressed in camouflage and holding rifles. They were grinning, as if they'd just shared an inside joke.

Kate stared at the picture. "Is that Wheatly on the end?"

"Yes." Mack's hand began to tremble, and he forced himself to still. What he was looking at had to be a hallucination because it didn't add up. He couldn't reconcile what he was seeing versus what he knew.

"Who are the other two guys?" Kate asked.

"I don't know the one in the middle. But this guy—" Mack pointed to a slim man with a military haircut standing on the far left "—this guy is my father."

He'd posted a phone number.

Kate's gaze fixed on the ten digits on the screen, while she debated what to do. She'd come home from searching Wheatly's house with Mack, who'd gone silent after finding the photo of his father with Wheatly and another man. She'd asked him a few questions, but he'd had little for answers. "I'm stunned," he'd said. "I don't know what to think."

Mack had told her on the ride back that his father had never mentioned knowing Wheatly, and especially not that the criminal was once a hunting buddy. Fordham was a small town, yes, but the chances of Wheatly, a petty criminal who barely held down jobs, and the decorated police detective being friends were pretty close to zero. Someone would have undoubtedly mentioned a connection like that.

"Kate, your pizza's getting cold," Jenn said as she came back from the kitchen with a slice of pepperoni for herself. She plopped down beside Kate and glanced at the screen. "Someone posted their phone number on your page? That's weird."

"It's from Wary Watcher. He wants to talk to me."

"Wait, back up." Jenn set the plate on the end table

and turned to face Kate. Concern knitted her brows. "Who is Wary Watcher, and why on earth would you talk to him? Not to mention, where were you this afternoon? I thought we were going to binge the new season of *Bridgerton*."

"I guess we have a lot to get caught up on." Kate closed the lid on her laptop and settled back on the couch. She'd been leaving Jenn in the dark on purpose to avoid the conversation they were about to have where Kate admitted—again—that she'd done some dangerous things, all in the name of finding the truth. After the day Kate sat in Wheatly's driveway and was saved from what could have been a life-threatening confrontation by the arrival of the police, Jenn had worried and stressed. She'd made Kate promise to never ever do such a thing again. When Kate made the promise, she'd meant it, but now...

She was so close to the truth. She could feel it, almost smell it, taste it, touch it. One or two more clues and everyone would have answers.

"So the last thing you told me," Jenn said, "was that they found Lily's body near where her car had been left. What's happened since then? And what does any of that have to do with someone leaving their phone number on your page?"

"It seems like a thousand things have happened, and it's only been a day." Had it really only been twenty-four hours since Lily's skeleton was discovered? So much had unraveled, so many new clues unearthed. The question was whether any of it meant anything.

Kate told Jenn about the discovery of the lighter at the crime scene, then their visit to Wheatly's abandoned house. "That photo was really weird, because it seemed like the elder Snyder was friends with Wheatly, but if that was so, I never saw any indication of that when he arrested him or when he testified against Wheatly in court."

"That is really weird. Maybe it was just a onetime thing, and the guy in the middle was the common friend?" Jenn took a bite of pizza. "You need to find out who the third guy was."

"Mack's looking into that right now."

"So it's Mack now, huh?" Jenn grinned. "Does this mean you might have a crush on the handsome detective and that maybe there's a second date in the works?"

"He hasn't mentioned it." Kate shrugged, feigning nonchalance. "And the first date was really more of a working dinner. I don't think he's interested in me like that anyway."

A little ribbon of disappointment underscored her words. She'd started to really care about the determined, reasonable detective. He invaded her thoughts a hundred times during the day, and with nearly everything she saw, read or said, she wondered what Mack would think about the same thing. And most of all, whether he was thinking of her, too, at that exact moment.

"Kate, he's a cop," Jenn said. "They like to do things

on their own, without any interference from anyone else, especially John Q. Public, which I think means he's not taking you out just because he wants to work with you. He's taken you along on every step of this investigation, sought your opinion many times and found reasons to spend time with you. I'd say he's doing that for more than just a little company while he drives over to Piedmont."

"Well, maybe." If Kate allowed the seeds of joy in her to take root, she'd think about nothing but Mack. If he didn't feel the same way, there would be nothing but heartache on the other side of those daydreams. "Either way, we don't have time for that. We have a murder to solve."

Jenn covered Kate's hand with her own. "Then there'll be another murder, and another after that. At some point, you have to have a personal life again."

"I do. Sort of."

"I'm no expert, but I'd say everything you're doing is avoiding having a personal life. Being busy from the minute you get up until you go to bed. Only discussing work stuff with your friends and someone you might be interested in but are pretending you're not..." Jenn shrugged. "Just saying."

There was too much at stake for Kate to set all that aside and start dating. Her romantic life could wait until after Lily's murderer was in prison.

Even as she thought those words, Kate knew Jenn had a point. If there was one thing she excelled at doing, it was avoiding her emotions for as long as possible. The first season of the podcast had forced her to deal with her grief, right there on the show. It had been painful, and at some points, torturous, but she had done it and emerged stronger from the experience. Now maybe it was time to start thinking about emotions besides loss.

"I guess I'm terrified of losing someone else," Kate said. "What if I do fall in love and then he—" a sob caught in her throat and forced the last word out on a whisper "—dies?"

"Hon, we all die someday. God doesn't want you living in the what-ifs. He wants you to live in the right now."

"You're right. I know you are. I'm just...scared."

"You?" Jenn grinned. "You are the bravest person I know. The craziest, but the bravest." The two of them laughed and the mood in the room lightened. "So what was up with the phone number on your show page?"

"That's from someone who's been commenting." The shift back to work talk redirected Kate to more familiar ground and away from all these feelings she didn't know what to do with yet. "He goes by the handle Wary Watcher. I don't know who he is, but he says he has evidence I need to hear about."

"You don't think it's Wheatly, do you?"

Kate shook her head. "I checked with Mack, and Wheatly doesn't have internet access in prison. Plus, the messages are different than what Wheatly sends me. I also ran a google search on the phone number when it came up on my page, and it's one of those prepaid phones that aren't traceable to a person."

"Whoa, whoa. Back up. Wheatly sends you messages?"

"Just a couple letters." She glanced away. "And a couple phone calls."

"Kate, I thought we talked about risking your life for this show. It's not worth it. You're not going to call this Wary Watcher, are you?"

She ran a finger along the rim of her glass, watching the liquid inside swirl against the sides. "I need to know what he knows."

"He's probably just a crackpot who's messing with you."

"But what if he isn't?" Kate leaned closer to Jenn. "What if he knows who killed Lily?"

"I know how much those answers mean to you, and I also realize if I tell you not to contact him, you're going to do it anyway. I just don't think you should do any of this alone ever again. If he is a killer, he could kill you, Kate." Jenn nibbled on her lower lip, her gaze going between the closed laptop and Kate's face. "If you call him, put him on speaker so we both can hear him. And you have to promise you're going to tell Mack about him right away."

Mack would kill her if he found out she'd called the person who'd threatened her on the show's page. He wanted her to be careful, to think through things before acting. In Kate's mind, Mack was too cautious. He walked all around a problem before he chose an angle of attack. Kate preferred to leap in and figure it out later. That approach had worked well before, with a killer in jail. Maybe it could work again.

She tugged her phone out of her pocket. "Okay, let's do it."

Jenn scooched closer. She met Kate's gaze and gave her a nod. Kate plugged in the numbers, then hit the green button to call. The number rang twice, then a husky voice said, "Why hello, Kate. You got my message and are finally responding. You have ignored every message I've posted until this one."

"There are a lot of people who post on that page."

"But none of them have the evidence I have." His voice was deep, gravelly, with a hint of laughter at the edges of his words, like he was playing a game and she was the unlucky pawn about to be sacrificed for the checkmate. "Evidence I am sure you are interested in seeing."

Jenn mouthed, *Then why doesn't he go to the police?*

"Why aren't you taking this evidence to the police?"

Wary Watcher chuckled. "Because the police already know me, and they aren't going to believe me. They have reasons to cover their tracks and make sure I stay forgotten."

"What reasons?"

"Tsk, tsk, Kate. You know I can't just tell you that. But I can show you. I know who killed Lily Ridge. I know who left that lighter in the woods."

Kate froze. The NCSBI had not released the information about the lighter to the public. Kate hadn't mentioned it on her show. As far as she knew, the only people who knew about it were Mack, herself, the police—and the man who dropped it. Wheatly? Or Wary Watcher? "Who is it? Tell me, and I'll make sure your story gets on the show."

He chuckled again, a chilling sound that sent shivers down Kate's spine. "Always in such a hurry to get the truth, aren't you, Kate? You need to learn patience or you're going to get yourself killed, sitting in the driveway of a killer." Another laugh, as if the whole thing was just one big joke. "I'll tell you what you want to know but only in person and not on some device you can record me with. I don't want you using our conversation to get yourself higher ratings."

Jenn was shaking her head so fast, her ponytail tapped her cheeks. "Don't do it. You can't trust him," she whispered.

"I don't think meeting in person is a good idea," Kate said.

"Then I don't have any information for you. It was nice chatting with you, Kate. This is our last conversation. When I hang up this phone, the information I have goes with me because I'm not here to play games. You have five seconds to make up your mind. Are you brave or are you a coward with a microphone? Five."

Kate looked at Jenn. Jenn was mouthing *No, no, no*.

"Four."

"Just give me a second!" Kate couldn't lose this connection and all the information he had. Wary

Watcher knew about the lighter and that alone made him an insider with the case. What if he knew who the killer—

"Three."

Jenn grabbed Kate's arm and shook her head even harder.

"Two."

"Wait!" she shouted before he could hang up. It was crazy, dangerous, and Mack was going to be furious, but she couldn't just let this guy slip away. Not until she had more information about him, enough to call the police. Even as she thought that, Kate was aware she was just repeating the same foolish mistakes she'd made with Wheatly. She'd be more careful this time, though, she vowed. Less foolhardy. "I'll meet you. When and where?"

"No time like the present. How about at our mutual friend John David Wheatly's house in twenty minutes? No cops, no one else, or I'll run. See you soon, Kate." The connection went dead.

And there it was. She might as well be stepping back in time, going to Wheatly's again to flush a killer out of the woods. What had she just done?

"What are you thinking?" Jenn sprung off the couch. "You can't meet him. Call Mack right now. It's the job of the police to talk to people like him."

"You heard him. It has to be me and only me. No cops." Kate was already grabbing her shoes and slipping them on her feet. Foolish or not, there was no way Kate was going to let another killer get away. "I have to go now or I'll be late. And Jenn, you're not going to stop me. If someone else dies because I don't catch Lily's murderer, I could never live with myself."

Jenn considered her friend for a long moment. "Fine. But I'm coming with you and we're calling Mack from the car."

Mack spent a frustrating two hours in the Piedmont Correctional Facility without his phone or his gun, waiting on visitation with Wheatly. The day before, three prisoners had ganged up on another man in the yard and stabbed him to death before the guards could intervene. The crowd gathered around the murdered man scattered, with the three assailants caught in that mix. The prison had instituted a lockdown while they replayed the security footage and found the three suspects.

They'd finally interviewed and then put the suspects in solitary confinement late this afternoon, but the extended lockdown had caused everything else in the prison to run behind schedule. Mack's visit with Wheatly kept getting delayed because the warden wanted to make sure every inch of Piedmont was secure before allowing any of the prisoners to leave their cells. Mack could literally feel the time ticking away, like water going over a cliff.

Wheatly strolled into the visitor's room a little after six in the evening. Just as he had before, Wheatly shuffled his shackled feet across the floor, then sat on the metal stool. His hands were also shackled, which meant he had to hold the plastic phone with both hands and crane his neck to hear. "Where's your partner in crime?"

"It's just you and me today, Wheatly. I have two questions for you, and I want straight answers."

He scoffed. "What's in it for me? Why should I even waste a breath helping you?"

"I don't have a reason for you," Mack said. He'd decided on the way to the prison that the best way to deal with Wheatly was with the truth. Mack had always lived by a code of truth first, and that life motto had served him well. "If you were framed like you claim you were, helping me right now will go far with the judge when you present your appeal."

Wheatly's gaze narrowed. He assessed Mack, probably weighing if the cop's words could be trusted. "What are the questions?"

"Why was this—" Mack pulled out a photo of the lighter he'd found "—at the Lily Ridge murder scene?"

Wheatly muttered under his breath, then shook his head and spat on the floor beside his stool. "That, Detective, is someone trying to frame me for another murder I didn't commit."

"Seems awfully convenient that you are saying you were framed for a second murder." Mack saw the irritation in Wheatly's face and walked his words back. "Why would someone want to frame you?"

"Because all he cares about is covering his own tracks. He doesn't care if I rot in here the rest of my life."

"He who?" But Wheatly just shook his head.

"I want a deal, Detective, before I talk. Go get the DA for me and then we can chat."

Mack reached into his inside pocket and touched the second photo he'd brought. If he never showed it to Wheatly, he'd never have the confirmation he dreaded. He could just walk out of this prison, leave Wheatly to rot and go back to investigating petty thefts of stone bunnies. The NCSBI had control of the Ridge case anyway, and surely they'd eventually circle back to Wheatly and his connection to the killer. This wasn't Mack's problem.

Except it was. He thought of Grace Ridge's face, the heartbreak and pleading in her eyes. *Please look harder. Please ask more questions, even if the answers are painful.* And he knew he couldn't let this go, no matter what it cost him. Grace had been brave enough to confront the truth. Mack needed to be too.

Mack slapped the photo he had found in Wheatly's closet onto the stainless steel table. "You recognize that?"

"You searching my house? That's not even legal."

"The city took possession of your house because you haven't been paying your taxes. Technically, it's not yours anymore, and what you left behind is considered trash, which is perfectly legal to search."

Wheatly scowled. "Still doesn't seem right."

"Take it up with my boss." Mack tapped on the picture. "Who is the man in the middle?"

A slow, knowing smile spread across Wheatly's face. "Why, would you look at that nice family-and-friends photo. Well, not all of us were friends. Some were just family tagging along. Either way, that was a good day. We took down a big buck, dressed it in the field, split up the meat when we got back." Wheatly leaned back in the metal office chair and stretched his arms over his head. Mack fought the urge to pound on the glass and get him to talk. "I'm surprised you don't know who your father's friends are."

"Why should I know who this is?" His father wasn't friends with Wheatly. That kind of connection would have been public knowledge in a town this small. Why would Wheatly say that? Just to get under Mack's skin?

"Dear old Dad is the one with the answer, and you knew that before you even came to see me, but you're too afraid of confronting Mr. SuperCop. You're barking up the wrong tree, Detective. I'm not the one you want. Go ask Daddy who he was with when he shot that twelve-point buck." Wheatly called over his shoulder for the guard, then got to his feet and shuffled toward the door.

"That's all you're going to tell me?" Mack shouted. "Those aren't answers."

Wheatly just shrugged and disappeared behind the stainless steel door once again. Mack shoved the photos back into his pocket and then suffered a painstaking fifteen minutes to get back through security. As he retrieved his phone, the notifications screen lit up. Two missed calls from Kate and a text that said only Need.

There was little signal in the massive concrete structure, so Mack ran out of the prison and toward the parking lot. A storm rumbled overhead, spitting rain and sparking lightning. Mack dialed Kate's number, put his car into gear and peeled out of the parking lot, making the long drive back to Fordham.

On the other end, the phone went straight to voice mail. Mack tried again and got the same result. At a stoplight, he texted her back. Where are you? Are you okay?

No response. Mack called the police department and asked the front desk sergeant to send a patrol car out to do a wellness check on Kate at both her coffee shop and her apartment. While he drove as fast as he could on the rain-slicked roads, his stomach in a knot, toward the only person who would have the answer he needed.

Chapter Fourteen

There was no way out.

Kate had not only put her own life in danger, but also Jenn's, and now they were probably going to die. Just like Luke had. Just like Lily had. She had no doubt now that Elaine had somehow gotten caught up in all of this, and that Wary Watcher was the one who had pulled the trigger.

"You know what happens to the women who cross me, don't you?" Wary Watcher said, his voice low and dark. "The women who don't do what I want them to do—they end up dead." His threat sent a shiver up her spine. She should have been smarter and taken Jenn's advice. Called the police department, refused to meet Wary Watcher. Instead, she'd let her headstrong, foolish side rule, maybe at the cost of their lives. Mack hadn't answered her calls, and she'd never had a chance to tell him where she was. Why didn't she leave a voice mail? Drop a pin with her location? Do something smart instead of thinking she and Jenn could handle this?

Jenn's wide, terrified eyes met Kate's from across the room. There was duct tape over her mouth and zip ties binding her hands behind her back. She looked scared and in pain, and Kate was helpless to do anything. It had all happened so fast, and now, they were probably going to die.

Five minutes ago, Kate had pulled into Wheatly's driveway. At first, she'd thought the whole thing had been a wild goose chase because the house was still standing empty and there were no cars besides the junkers that were there before.

Then she saw a shadow out of the corner of her eye, a flicker of movement, and a man slipped out from behind a tree, sprinted to the car and pressed the barrel of a gun against the driver's side window before Kate could even react.

A ski mask covered his face. He was tall, over six feet, and at least two hundred pounds, she guessed, under all that hunter's camouflage. No wonder he had blended in so well with the woods. *Get out of the car. Now.*

Jenn shrieked. Behind them, Harley whined in the backseat and began to pace. Jenn put a hand on Kate's arm. "Kate, we can't do that! He'll kill us!"

"I know." Kate dropped the transmission into Reverse. Maybe she could gun it and—

He shot at the car and the front tire exploded with a loud bang, then another shot a split second later, and the rear tire was flat. Jenn and Kate screamed, and all thoughts of fleeing came to a stop. Harley barked and bounced around the back of the car, alternately growling at the man and barking at Kate.

"Get out of the car. Or I'll shoot you next. You've ruined everything by bringing someone else along. You were supposed to be alone, Kate. Alone." His words were even and soft, but so cold, they sent a spike of fear down Kate's back. She looked at Jenn, and the two of them whispered a quick *God, please help us*, before they unclipped their seat belts. Just before she slid out of the car, Kate tried to send a text to Mack, praying that he could somehow find her, but she only managed to send a single word before Harley knocked the phone out of her hands. He bounded over Kate and lunged for the man, but he raised the gun and fired at the dog.

Kate had screamed, "No! Harley!"

The dog yelped, a loud, painful sound, and the man raised the gun again. Harley managed to scramble into the woods, leaving a thick, dark trail of blood behind him. There was a rustle, and then the woods went silent. *Oh, God, not Harley. Please don't let him die*. She was the one who suggested bringing the dog as a sort of security against the stranger they were meeting, and now Harley, too, was caught in this just for being his loyal, wonderful self. Kate wanted to run after the dog but knew if she took a single step, Wary Watcher would shoot her as well.

"Cooperate and you won't end up like your dog." The man waved toward the cabin. "Now get moving."

Jenn was trembling so hard she stumbled as she tried to cross the dirt path. Kate reached for her friend and slipped an arm around her waist, helping her forward. "Jenn? You okay?" Lord forgive her for dragging her roommate into this mess. Why didn't she listen to Jenn? Why had she thought she could handle this?

"Don't speak! Either one of you." Wary Watcher glared at them, his eyes two pinholes peering out of a black ski mask. "Just do as you're told."

There were two of them and one of him, but even Kate knew that two women were no match for a man with a gun and excellent aim. She couldn't risk getting Jenn shot—*just like Harley. No, she couldn't think about that now*—and maybe dying. The only thing Kate knew to do was to keep Wary Watcher talking, because all he seemed to have been after these past few weeks was a conversation with her. Maybe she could plead her way out of this or at least buy enough time for Mack to find them.

Then she remembered Mack had gone to Piedmont today to talk to Wheatly. That meant he was at least three hours away, if he even figured out where they were. Kate closed her eyes and begged God for forgiveness for being so, so foolish.

"Why are you doing this?" Kate said. "You have to know that killing a member of the media will bring more heat on you."

He scoffed. "You think I don't know how to get away with murder?" He leaned down close—so close his breath was warm against her ear. "If only you had played along, we wouldn't be here. All I ever wanted was your attention, dear Kate."

Before she could reply, the man took them into the

cabin, shoved both of them down to the floor, then made Kate zip-tie Jenn. She tried to be loose with the restraints, but Wary Watcher checked her work. "Don't try anything stupid, Kate, or I'll shoot you both." He jerked the plastic bindings tighter, causing Jenn to cry out, then he slapped a piece of duct tape across Jenn's mouth.

"I'm so sorry, Jenn," Kate said, horrified that they were still in this situation. It was all her fault. "I'm so—"

Wary Watcher yanked Kate's arm behind her. "I said shut up." He took out a second zip tie and bound Kate's arms in the same way. He reached for the roll of duct tape and loomed over her.

"You…you…wanted me to hear your side of the story all this time," Kate said, faking a bravado she didn't feel. "You have my attention now. Talk to me."

He held the piece of tape in his hands and weighed what she had said. Finally, he set the tape on the battered kitchen table. He yanked Kate up by her bound arms, then set her down against the center post holding up a beam that traversed the ceiling. "You know, I've been watching you for months. For years, really."

Terror snaked through her. He had been watching her? She forced her voice to remain steady and calm. "Why?"

"You were so determined to solve the murder of that nosy pastor. I thought maybe you would appreciate my work, but you ignored everything I said."

"I… I'm sorry."

"I grew to care about you, Kate," he said, his voice

a harsh rasp. He rubbed the back of his hand across her cheek, knuckles skipping over her skin like a snake. "But you were just like the others. Ignoring me. Making me feel like a fool." He leaned in close, his eyes so dark they were almost black. "Now, we'll see who the fool really is."

Kate fought the urge to scream. They were far, far from civilization. No one would hear them cry for help. And worst of all, no one could come rescue them.

"She's not there. We checked both places, did a patrol through the town. No sign of her, Detective." The desk sergeant's words made Mack press the accelerator even harder. The rain had slowed, and he pushed the car as hard as he dared.

"Keep checking," Mack said, even though he knew they wouldn't find Kate. She wasn't at the grocery store or at a movie with her roommate. She was caught up in this mess somehow and very, very likely in danger.

Nevertheless, Mack did his own check of both her apartment and the coffee shop. The apartment was dark and empty, the coffee shop closed with no one inside. He stood in the street, rain misting his clothes. Where was she?

Need. What did she need? Answers? To see him? Or worse...did Kate need help?

Failure hung heavy over Mack. How could he have left her alone here? Headstrong Kate would have gone off investigating on her own, and Mack should have realized that. He deeply regretted not checking in with her more today and finding out her plans. Where could she be?

Dear old Dad. Mack thought of what Wheatly had said and realized this was the only clue he had. Somehow, Mack had to solve this crime right now, because that was the only way he was ever going to find Kate.

If he wasn't already too late.

His father stared at the photo for a long time. Then the defensiveness, the self-righteousness, and most of all, the fight, drained from his body. His shoulders sank, and he dropped into a kitchen chair. "Where did you find this?"

"In a box in Wheatly's closet." Mack didn't ask any questions. He simply waited for his father to fill in the blanks. He'd arrived on James's doorstep just as the storm broke overhead and soaked Fordham in a flash spring storm. His father had been watching TV when Mack arrived. He'd taken one look at his son's face, shut off the TV and gotten to his feet. Mack set the photo of Wheatly, his father and the mystery man down on the small table and waited for answers.

"This was a long time ago," James said. "More than thirty years." His father ran a hand through his close-cropped hair and let out a long sigh. "I suppose you want to know why I'm standing there with a killer and his brother."

"Wait…did you say that was Wheatly's brother?"

"Half-brother. Came with the second husband into the mom's life. He was five, six years older than John David."

"Closer to your age then." Which would make sense for why his father would be hanging around the man in the middle. But with Wheatly? A known criminal? In the photo, Mack's father was all of seventeen. Young and dumb, as Dad liked to put it. "Were you friends with him?"

"Not John David. He was just the annoying tag-along. But Garrett and I…yes, we were friends. He was the running back on the team. Could have had a future, if he hadn't gone down the wrong path." His father glanced away. "I guess you could say Garrett and I were friends."

"Garrett Wheatly." Mack searched his memory. "I've never heard his name. He must not live in town anymore."

James scoffed. "Garrett doesn't really live any-where. He's a long-haul trucker. On the road more than he's in a bed. He left town after he got into some…trouble after high school."

A sense of urgency pounded in Mack's veins. He kept thinking of that one-word text from Kate. He needed to find her, not rehash high school with his father. "I don't care where he's been or what he's been doing for a job. Would he be the type of person to frame Wheatly for another murder?"

James arched a brow. "You kidding me? Garrett would frame his own mother if it would get him out of trouble."

"And where is he now?" When his father didn't answer, Mack knew there was something James was leaving unsaid, something he clearly didn't want to tell his son. "Dad! Where is he? I need to know right now, and I have a feeling you've kept tabs on him over the years."

His father scowled, but in the end, he relented. "If he's not on the road, he's probably at Wheatly's house."

"But it's abandoned." Mack had just been there the other day. No one was living there. Except…there were those few cans in the kitchen that looked fairly new. Could Garrett have been using the empty house as a place to crash?

His father shrugged. "Garrett isn't one for caring about where he lays his head at night."

Mack snatched up the photo and stuffed it back into his jacket. It would take fifteen minutes to get to Wheatly's house from here. Fifteen minutes that Mack wasn't sure he had left. "I have to go. I think Garrett has taken Kate, and maybe her roommate too."

As he turned to go, his father grabbed his arm and stopped him. "We have a lot to talk about, son, but first, you have to let me come with you. Garrett isn't going to listen to anyone but me."

"Why?" What was his father hiding? And what did it have to do with Kate?

There was a long pause, then Dad shook his head and averted his gaze. "If I can get through this day without telling you that answer, I'll be forever grateful." James ducked into the passenger's side of Mack's car and shut the door. "I don't think that's going to happen. All shadows come into the light sometime, don't they?"

Mack didn't answer. He just drove. Fast.

The pain radiated from the top of Kate's shoulder, down into her shoulder blade and across her chest. Dull and achy until she tried to move or adjust the way she was sitting, then it was a razor-sharp pain that arced through her. Twice, she'd cried out, only to see the gun in front of her face. Three times, she'd bitten down on her lip, trying to stay silent. Across from her, Jenn sat ramrod straight, her face white with fear. *I'm sorry*, Kate mouthed.

Jenn's head moved in an almost imperceptible nod. Tears welled in her eyes, and Kate knew she had to do something or they were both going to die. She'd tried to keep Wary Watcher talking, but he'd eventually gotten annoyed and told her to shut up. It seemed like hours had passed since then, as a storm rumbled through, soaked the ground and then dried to just a few droplets pinging off the metal roof.

"Who are you?" she asked.

The question made Wary Watcher leap forward, crouch on his knees and press the gun under her chin. Cold, hard metal rubbed against her skin, menacing and lethal. "You don't get to ask the questions. I told you that. You're just like all the others, thinking you can boss me around. I make the rules here, not you."

"But you promised me answers. You said all

you've ever wanted is to talk with me, so I could see the work you had done." She raised her chin and tried her best to look fearless. "The least you can do is finish telling me everything before you kill me."

"Curiosity is what killed the cat, you know. You should stop being so curious." All she could see was his eyes, those deadly, dark, glittering eyes, peering out of the mask. "It can be a deadly vice."

"At least let me see your face," she said. "I want to know who is shooting me before I die."

He tugged off the ski mask and tossed it onto the kitchen table. Then he bent down before Kate and gave her a terrifying grin. "There. Now you've seen my face. You know that means I definitely have to kill you both, right?"

Jenn started shrieking under the duct tape and stomping her feet against the floor. Kate willed Jenn to calm down, to trust her in this situation. She wiggled her fingers behind her back and out of the corner of her eye, she saw Jenn give a quick nod before settling down again.

"I already know who you are," Kate said to Wary Watcher. This was a man who wanted attention, she realized. A man who wanted to think he had the upper hand at all times. Maybe if she turned those tables a little it would knock him off-balance. "I've seen your picture. Twice."

"Twice? And where do you think you've seen me? Because I ain't no cover model, Miss Nosy."

"You were the bus driver." She hadn't been certain before she said it, but as she spoke the words, she saw his face in the picture of the youth group retreat. He was standing on the bus step, his wide frame filling the door. He had the same shaggy graying hair and the same scruffy beard that day as he had now. She remembered Luke saying something about the bus company being contracted, using part-time employees for the occasional summer job. "And you've been in my coffee shop."

He'd always worn a ball cap and sat in the far corner. He'd had a beard then, too, and she hadn't made the connection until now because he'd been one of dozens of customers coming in for their morning coffee. Always during the rush times, never lingering as the shop emptied out. *I've been watching you. For years.*

She'd been too wrapped up in everything else to notice this man. And now, it was going to cost her not only her own life but Jenn's too.

"Well aren't you the clever one?" Wary Watcher turned toward Jenn, swiveling the gun with the movement. Jenn pushed with her feet, pressing harder into the wall, trying to put even a millimeter of distance between herself and the barrel of the gun. "She's pretty smart, isn't she?"

"Don't talk to her," Kate said, almost shouting the words, desperate to bring his attention back to her. "She doesn't know anything."

"And what, you have all the answers?" He slowly pivoted back to Kate. Instead of pointing the gun at her, he set it on his knee but kept his finger on the trigger. If she could just get him to put the gun down, maybe she could tackle him or something.

"I have some of the answers." She shifted forward, even though the movement made her shoulders scream in agony. The pieces had started falling into place on the drive over here, as she thought about the postings on the show's page, what Ashley had told her and the clues Kate and Mack had unearthed. It all made sense now, even if all of it had resulted in many senseless deaths. "You had a thing for Lily. Followed her home from work, tried to talk to her, but she wanted nothing to do with you. Then you got the job as the bus driver for the retreat. Lily realized who you were and confided in Luke and maybe he confronted you because that's what Luke would do, which meant he…" She pushed the words out, barely skipping a beat even though the words hurt as much as her shoulder. "Had to be killed."

"Your boyfriend wasn't so chivalrous, Kate. No, he didn't confront me. He made sure he spent a lot of time talking to Lily alone. Right under my nose. She wouldn't look at me after that." Wary Watcher's face reddened and his jaw hardened. "Lily was perfect and beautiful, and she would have been mine if he didn't interfere."

"You didn't have to kill her."

"Oh, but I did. She went with me willingly at first, but then she started screaming and trying to run away from me. I had to stop her. Just like I stopped him."

"And Elaine too." She didn't even have to ask it as

a question. Like everything else, it made sense that Elaine Reynolds had gotten caught in the crossfire of this sick man's twisted game.

"Poor Elaine. Such a pretty girl, but so sad all the time." He rocked back on his heels. "She always remembered me and looked forward to my visits. Every time I went to the diner, Elaine would hurry to make sure I had my favorite meal right away."

Kate could see the pattern now. He'd fall for a girl, delude himself into thinking she felt the same and when the woman rebuffed him, he killed her. "And you thought that meant she had fallen for you."

"She did. I know she did." He leaned in and his foul breath nearly made Kate gag. She tried to scoot back but there was nowhere to go from her place on the floor. "She would have been mine, but then she started talking about Lily. She was calling me all these names, and I simply couldn't hear those ugly words come out of her pretty mouth. So I took care of her too."

"Elaine never did anything to hurt you. Lily was just a kid. And Luke…" Kate shook her head. "Why couldn't you have left them alone?"

Wary Watcher tsk-tsked, as if he'd been caught stealing a cookie before dinner, not recounting a string of murders. "You're just like the rest of them. Full of questions. I don't answer to them. I don't answer to anyone."

You'll answer to God, she thought but didn't say.

"She wasn't the first, and she won't be the last." He grinned at his own humor of using the lines he'd posted on the show's page. "Clever of me to say it like that, wasn't it? I could have been talking about any of the women I've killed. I'm smarter than you think, little radio bird. Much smarter."

"I'm sure you are." Appealing to his ego seemed to be the only way to get him to open up. She had to make him think he could trust her, so that he would let down his guard. "You got away with three murders for years."

"And so many more. It's too bad, really, that you had to start investigating me. Now, we can't be together. It's all your fault, nosy girl." He reached forward, grabbed her shirt by the collar and yanked her halfway off the floor. Kate cried out in pain, and tears began to stream down her face. "Because now I'm about to add two more murders to the total. And they won't catch me for these either because I'll be on the road long before your little cop friend even realizes you're missing. In and out of town, like a shadow."

He cocked the gun and pressed it to her left temple—he was a lefty, she realized and knew that knowledge wouldn't matter when she was dead—but before he could pull the trigger, there was a shuffling sound, then something whooshed past her, and Wary Watcher tumbled to the ground, releasing Kate. She landed hard on her left shoulder, the pain exploding behind her eyes.

As the pain ebbed a degree, her vision began to clear. She saw Harley on top of Wary Watcher, with his jaw clamped around the man's shoulder. Harley was bleeding from a wound on his right hip, but he didn't let go. Wary Watcher was screaming at the dog to get off as he thrashed about the floor and Harley, God bless him, held on for dear life. Kate scooted back until she was against the wall, pressing her heels into the floor until she could begin to rise.

Then the gun went off, and Kate crumpled to the floor.

Chapter Fifteen

Just as he reached Wheatly's driveway, Mack heard the unmistakable crack of a gunshot. He slammed the car into Park, then scrambled out the door, his father only a couple steps behind him. "Call for backup," he screamed at his father, as he ran the fastest he'd ever run in his life. The journey from driveway to inside Wheatly's house—a matter of maybe thirty feet—seemed to take thirty years. In that excruciating space of time, Mack prayed.

Don't let Kate die. Please let me get there in time. Please protect her and Jenn.

Then he was through the door, and in the middle of the chaos, he saw Kate. She was a puddle on the floor, with a spreading pool of crimson underneath her. Jenn was across the room, curled into a ball, her face turned toward the wall while she sobbed. Harley lay in the opposite corner, wounded and panting.

But the man—the man was right beside Kate, his gun pointed down at her temple. From this angle,

Mack couldn't tell if she was dead or alive. *Please be alive*, he prayed. *Please, God, don't let her die.*

"I would put down that gun if I were you," the other man said. He was tall and lean, with a three-day scruff and longish graying hair, but the face was the same. Garrett Wheatly, looking meaner and rougher than he had in that photo thirty-odd years ago. He was also armed and clearly not afraid to shoot. "If you don't put your gun down, Detective, this isn't going to end well for you or your girlfriend here."

"You're not dumb enough to shoot a cop. It's over. Just put down the weapon." Mack held his gun, steady and calm, the barrel aimed dead center on Garrett's head. He shifted a step forward. Behind him, he could hear his father, just outside the cabin, maybe casing the building or waiting for the right moment to pounce. Mack didn't know and didn't care. Every ounce of his concentration was narrowed on the barrel of Garrett's gun.

"You're not going to shoot me," Garrett said with a little half smile that made Mack's blood run cold. "Because you don't want your little radio bird to die. And I'll kill her if you so much as blink."

"Garrett, it's over. Just put the gun down." James emerged from behind Mack, with his own weapon in his hand. He shifted to stand beside his son, a few inches taller, but still in the same stance and steady grip on his weapon. "Let the girls go and let's all walk out of here."

"Like you did all those years ago?" Garrett scoffed.

"I don't think so, James. I took the rap for you once. I'm not doing it again."

"What is he talking about?" Mack asked. He moved a few inches to the right, trying to see if Kate was moving. Jenn gave him an *I don't know* look of fear and sorrow. In the back of the room, Harley was whining in pain.

"My, my, Detective," Garrett said. "I take it you don't know about your daddy's escapades as a teenager?"

"Garrett, shut up." James growled the words and took a step closer to the shooter. "Stop. Talking."

Kate moaned, and relief flooded Mack. She was alive, and if he could get her an ambulance, she would be okay. But her moan made Garrett draw her closer to his chest, using her as a shield, blocking any shot Mack could take. "Your girlfriend should hear this, too, don't you think? And, Detective, if you're thinking you can get me to keep talking until your backup shows, you're wrong. Dear old Dad here didn't call for backup. He doesn't want anyone hearing his stories. Isn't that right, Jimmy?"

"Let her go, Garrett." James raised his gun, moved it left, right, but with the small room and Kate between them, he couldn't get a clear shot either.

"Jimmy, you don't get to decide what happens here. Not anymore." Garrett rose to his feet, dragging Kate with him. She let out little yelps of pain as he jerked her around, and Mack fought the urge to kill the man right now because doing that would risk Kate too much.

Mack's finger itched against the trigger and sweat beaded on his brow. Garrett was keeping Kate tight to his chest, her head close to his. There was no room for a clean shot. No opportunity that wouldn't risk hurting Kate. Blood ran down her side, staining her shirt, her jeans.

"You should have gone to prison after that accident, not me." Garrett's voice seethed with resentment and pent-up hatred. "You're the one who went after that kid in the bar fight with a pipe and hit him over the head before you ran like the chicken you are. That's premeditation right there, going to get the pipe and chasing after that kid who was just flirting with your girl. That kid would have died, except I scooped him up and brought him to the hospital. And what'd that little Good Samaritan act get me? Arrested."

"Garrett, shut up!"

The other man turned his attention to Mack and kept talking, as if James hadn't spoken. "Then your dear old dad here comes and offers me a deal. I take the hit and serve his time, and he gives me ten grand for a new start when I get out. In exchange, he gets to become Cop of the Year. You see, he had just gotten hired with the Fordham PD when he hit that kid, and that would have looked mighty bad on his résumé, wouldn't it? So I got to become a convicted felon. It wasn't so bad. Not as bad as my childhood. At least I got a bed and three meals a day, and ten grand to keep my mouth shut."

"You're not keeping it shut now," Dad said. "I'm telling you, Garrett, to quit talking."

"You've been doing all the talking for too long, Jimmy. Then I got into a little trouble of my own when that do-gooder pastor tried to keep me away from my girl. So I called on my old pal Jimmy to cover it up for me. You owed me, didn't you? You were glad to help that evidence disappear over and over and over again. Three times, you've repaid that debt, and you know what? It ain't nearly enough times."

"I'm done with you," James said. "I should have let you go to prison again."

"And then where would you be? I think they take away your Cop of the Year award when you're convicted of aiding and abetting. I hope you cleaned all your fingerprints off that pastor's car before you dropped it in my brother's yard. You cleaned up after me, every single time. Just like my little brother used to. He idolized me and wanted to be just like me. Followed me around like a needy puppy clinging to my leg. Now he is just like me, isn't he? Rotting away in jail, taking the fall for his big brother, thanks to your help, Jimmy boy." Garrett whipped his gun up and pointed it at James. "Maybe you should be the one to take the fall for my little radio bird and her friend and your nosy son. Then we'll call it square."

Two things happened at the same time—Kate's gaze met Mack's, and in that unspoken connection they had had from the very first day, she dipped her head toward Garrett's opposite side and Mack shot. The slug hit Garrett square in the temple, and he stumbled back, firing as he crashed to the floor.

Mack saw his father collapse, but then Kate was falling, and Mack scooped her up just before she hit the floor. She was pale and wide-eyed, but she was alive, and for that, he was so grateful to God. "Are you okay?" he asked.

"Yes, yes. I'm fine."

She was anything but fine, and they both knew it. The bleeding from her side seemed to have slowed so he cut the bindings on her wrists and then handed her his pocketknife. She crawled over to Jenn. Next, Mack crossed the room to check that Garrett was dead. There was no light in Garrett Wheatly's eyes, but Mack kicked his gun away just to be safe. He pulled out his cell as he hurried to his father's side, pressing 9-1-1 and shouting directions into the phone.

James was ashen, and his breathing was shallow. He'd been hit in the chest, too close to his heart, and the spreading puddle of blood said there wasn't likely to be a second miracle tonight. "I'm sorry, son."

"You're going to be all right, Dad. Just hold on." Mack willed it to be true, even as he watched a crimson path that told a different story. "I called an ambulance."

"I'm sorry I didn't tell you about—" he cast his gaze away "—about my past."

Or the fact that his father, a much-praised detective, had tampered with three investigations just to cover up a mistake he'd made. Three families had gone to sleep at night without all the facts, without the truth, because James Snyder had cared more about his career than their pain. How many times had his father protected a friend? That brotherhood he'd had on the football team had cost so many people far too much.

Mack had plenty he wanted to say to his father about all of that, but he could see the light fading from James's eyes, the fight draining from him with each passing second. So Mack sat beside him, held his hand and whispered words of forgiveness, because that was all the two of them had.

James Snyder died just as the sirens began wailing up the mountain. Mack gave his father one final hug, then crossed to Kate and Jenn. The two of them were huddled together, embracing and crying, their bodies turned away from the two dead bodies on the floor of John David Wheatly's cabin.

It was over. But Mack had a feeling that the questions were just getting started.

Kate stepped outside her apartment, closed her eyes for a second and inhaled until she'd filled her lungs with the fragrance of home. It had been a month since the day in the cabin, and every single moment had reminded her of how lucky she had been and how grateful she was to God for sending Mack to that cabin in time.

Harley came out behind Kate, pressing his long body against her leg, his tail thumping a beat of love. He'd been shot in the flank, and after a harrowing surgery, he'd recovered quite well. There'd been a lot of extra dog treats for Harley after he got home from the vet, each one a reward for bravery from a dog who did his best.

Jenn hurried down the stairs, a cup of coffee in one hand and her keys in the other. She'd had a hard time sleeping after all they had been through, and this time, Kate got to be the supportive shoulder for Jenn to cry on. Gradually, their lives had returned to normal and Jenn was mostly back to her regular cheery self.

"I'm late, as usual." She gave Kate a quick hug. "Have fun with your own personal hero today."

"He's not my…" Kate blushed. "Whatever he is, well, it's undefined."

"Give it time. I guarantee that handsome cop is going to put a lifetime definition on what he feels when he looks at you." Jenn grinned, then waved and hopped in her car.

A second later, Mack pulled into the driveway, giving Jenn a beep as she passed his sedan. He jumped out, then opened the passenger's side door for Kate. The sun was just starting to crest over the mountain by her building, casting a soft glow on his handsome features. He'd spent two weeks tying up all the loose ends after Garrett Wheatly died and then helping the families of Luke, Elaine and Lily gain closure. The coroner had been charged with covering up James's crimes, an announcement that had made everything Mack's father did become public knowledge. Mack's reputation had suffered a small ding, until Chief Richmond talked to the media, praising the detective's selfless handling of the investigation.

Sunday night, they'd all held a memorial vigil for the three people whose lives had been lost much too soon. Kate set up a fund-raiser on her show's page to send more troubled teens to the youth camp and to help fund additional mental health services in town. Her followers had already donated twenty thousand dollars to the Lily & Elaine Journey Fund, which meant several people would get to have their lives changed by giving, caring people like Luke Winslow.

"You know, you really don't have to drive me to work every day," she said to Mack. Every time he was with her, everything seemed brighter, warmer, happier. She realized she'd missed him in the few hours they'd been apart. "I can drive myself again. Garrett is dead, Wheatly is working on his appeal and my podcast is taking a much-needed break."

"I know." He grinned. "But I like seeing you first thing every morning."

"I like seeing you first thing in the morning too," she admitted. "I like it a lot."

He leaned on the open door and met her gaze with his own. "Think maybe we should do something about that?"

Harley gave his owner one more tail wag, then bounded off toward the fenced-in yard. Kate had installed a new lock on the fence, as well as a dog door that only Harley's collar could open. Even though Garrett was dead, she figured a little extra precaution couldn't hurt. "Do something like what?" Kate said as she closed the gate and gave Harley a wave.

"Like fall in love, get married, have a bunch of kids and solve crimes in our spare time?" Mack said.

She stopped in the middle of the driveway and stared at him. Had she heard Mack right? "You want to…fall in love?"

"Well, honestly, I think I already did that." He pushed off from the door and took three giant strides, bringing him almost nose-to-nose with Kate. He took both her hands in his, and she realized how right his touch felt, how perfect, as if they'd always been meant to be together.

The last few weeks had been a whirlwind of talking to the police, doing media interviews and wrapping up season three of her podcast, but Kate and Mack had made time to see each other. At first, he'd said it was because he wanted to make sure she was okay, after she was shot in the side. But the shot had been a through-and-through, and Kate had been out of the hospital by the next morning. She'd been back to normal a few days later—not exactly a reason to need a worried cop on her doorstep all the time.

But Mack kept coming by every single day, and they'd fallen into a comfortable, wonderful routine of starting the day with each other. He'd talk about cold cases he wanted to investigate, and she'd toss out ideas for the next season of the podcast, but inevitably the conversation would ebb and flow as it always did around their faith and their dreams for the future. And somewhere in the midst of all that, their friendship had developed into something more.

Something more…like love? She could hardly believe he'd said the word and almost wanted to have him repeat it just so she could be sure.

"So, is me telling you that I love you a bad thing?" Mack asked as they wandered out of the driveway and up the steep mountain road beside her building. "Because you're not saying anything and I have to admit, I'm a little worried I didn't make a strong enough case for myself."

She smiled. A rush of joy ran from her head to her toes. She'd never thought she could ever be this happy again, but here she was, with a rich, full life that was framed with gratitude and faith. "I think you falling in love with me is a wonderful thing, Mack. I... I had no idea you felt that way."

"Well, I was waiting to see if there was enough evidence to prove you felt the same way too." He tipped her chin with his finger. "Is there enough evidence, Ms. McAllister?"

"To prove I love you?" At the crest of the hill, Kate stepped closer to Mack, so close he could kiss her if he just leaned his head a few inches. "I think you can see the answer in my eyes."

"I see my whole world in your eyes, Kate," he said, as he drew her tight to his chest. "And my whole future."

"Then what should we do about that?"

"The only thing we can do." He pressed a kiss to her temple and whispered against the kiss, "Spend the rest of our lives together."

"That sounds like the best ending I could have ever hoped for." Kate stood on the top of the mountain with Mack and watched the sun finish its journey from slumber to shine. There would be time for coffee and work later. For now, there was just them.

* * * * *

LOVE INSPIRED

Stories to uplift and inspire

Fall in love with Love Inspired—
inspirational and uplifting stories of faith
and hope. Find strength and comfort in
the bonds of friendship and community.
Revel in the warmth of possibility and the
promise of new beginnings.

Sign up for the Love Inspired newsletter
at **LoveInspired.com** to be the first
to find out about upcoming titles,
special promotions and exclusive content.

CONNECT WITH US AT:

Facebook.com/LoveInspiredBooks

Twitter.com/LoveInspiredBks

Get 4 FREE REWARDS!

We'll send you 2 FREE Books plus 2 FREE Mystery Gifts.

FREE
Value Over
$20

Both the **Love Inspired®** and **Love Inspired® Suspense** series feature compelling novels filled with inspirational romance, faith, forgiveness, and hope.

HARLEQUIN
PLUS

Announcing a **BRAND-NEW** multimedia subscription service for romance fans like you!

Read, Watch and Play.

Experience the easiest way to get the romance content you crave.

Start your **FREE 7 DAY TRIAL** at
<u>www.harlequinplus.com/freetrial</u>.

IF YOU ENJOYED THIS BOOK
WE THINK YOU WILL ALSO LOVE

LOVE INSPIRED
INSPIRATIONAL ROMANCE

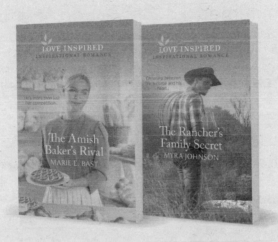

Uplifting stories of faith, forgiveness and hope.

Fall in love with stories where faith helps
guide you through life's challenges, and discover
the promise of a new beginning.

6 NEW BOOKS AVAILABLE EVERY MONTH!

LIXSERIES2021

SPECIAL EXCERPT FROM

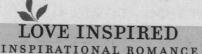

LOVE INSPIRED
INSPIRATIONAL ROMANCE
MOUNTAIN RESCUE

*When a blizzard traps federal witness Kiera Driscoll
and her seven-month-old daughter in the mountains,
she has no choice but to trust that Nash Myers will
keep them safe. But as the storm closes in, so do the
threats to her life…*

Read on for a sneak preview of
Blizzard Refuge,
by New York Times *bestselling author Cathy McDavid.*

"Is that a tree?" Kiera asked.

"Yeah, buried in the snowbank," Marshal Gifford replied. "Must be what we hit."

It was then the acute hopelessness of their situation sank in. They were trapped. And it would be dark soon. "What's going to happen to us?"

"Don't panic."

How could she not? Even if Marshal Gifford managed to start the car, they weren't going anywhere. Not without a tow truck or a Good Samaritan. And unless the storm abated, neither was a possibility. While Marshal Gifford rummaged through the glove compartment and her travel bag, Kiera held a bottle of formula in her hands, attempting to warm it. Heather wasn't hungry, but Kiera needed something to occupy herself or she'd lose her wits.

They were going be all right, she told herself over and over. God wouldn't abandon her and Heather, not after they'd come this far. He'd send help. She need only have faith.

Five minutes stretched into ten and then thirty.

"I see something!" Marshal Gifford pressed her face to the driver's side window.

Kiera stared, too, though her view was obstructed.

"There's a vehicle coming toward us."

Indeed, a silver shape materialized in the blinding snow. "It's a truck," Kiera said, her bones turning to jelly. They were going to be rescued.

"Stay quiet," Marshal Gifford ordered. "Let me do the talking." Dread filled Kiera as she realized her mistake. Rather than being rescued, they might be in grave peril. This could well be one of the 7-Crowns Syndicate's operatives sent to eliminate her.

"Remember our cover story."

Kiera swallowed. *Cover story. Right. Think.*

She silently reminded herself of the details and watched, with a mix of trepidation and excitement, as the truck came to a stop a few feet in front of them. The driver's side door opened, and a tall man emerged. He wore a bright blue winter parka, and a cowboy hat sat on his head over a pair of earmuffs. He'd wound a red scarf around his neck, concealing his face from the eyes down.

Friend or foe? Kiera couldn't tell, and her pulse raced.

Suddenly, she saw it. The vivid green Christmas wreath with a big red bow affixed to the front of the truck.

Always a believer in signs, she was ready to accept that God had sent her one. This man, whoever he was, would rescue them.

Marshal Gifford was clearly less convinced and removed the Glock from her shoulder harness hidden beneath her jacket.

Don't miss
Blizzard Refuge *by Cathy McDavid,*
available October 2022 wherever
Love Inspired books and ebooks are sold.

LoveInspired.com

**IF YOU ENJOYED THIS BOOK
WE THINK YOU WILL ALSO LOVE**

LOVE INSPIRED
INSPIRATIONAL ROMANCE
MOUNTAIN RESCUE

Courage. Danger. Faith.

Find strength and determination in stories
of faith and love in the face of danger.

AVAILABLE SEPTEMBER 27, 2022